"Ethan nervously watched as Currant created a new heart for Zak."
X-ooming FDR 1934   Frontispiece (p. 183)

Time Travel Twins

X-ooming FDR 1934

W. Green

ZIPPY BOOKS®

VELOCITER - SECURUS - ERUDITIO

Time Travel Twins: X-ooming FDR 1934 by W. Green
Copyright © 2017, 2022 William R. Green.
All rights reserved

Published by Zippy Books
822-607-207- ZippyBooks.com

Frontispiece Illustration by Nebojsa Pejic

ISBN-13: 978-0-9981623-2-4
(Zippy Books)

In Memory of George W. Peacher, Jr.

———————————————

TIME TRAVEL TWINS
By W. Green

SAVING JFK

X-OOMING FDR-1932

X-OOMING FDR-1933

X-OOMING FDR-1934

SAVING TRUMP

-Zippy Books-

CONTENTS

Sworn testimony before the U.S. House of Representatives, Special Committee on Un-American Activities, Investigation of Nazi Propaganda Activities and Investigation of Certain Other Propaganda Activities, United States Congress, November 1934.

As questioned by Congressman John W. McCormack, Chairman

Testimony of General Smedley Butler, United States Marines Ret.

Answer: *"I think I had probably better go back and give you the background. This has been going on for a year and a half. Along—I think it must have been about the 1st of July 1933, two men came to see me. First, there was a telephone message from Washington, from a man who I did not know well. His first name was* **Jack**. *He was an American Legionnaire, but I cannot remember his last name—cannot recall it now accurately. Anyhow, he asked me if I would receive 2 soldiers—2 veterans—if they called on me that afternoon. I said I would."*

Testimony of Gerald C. MacGuire, Bond Salesman for Grayson M-P Murphy & Company

Question: *"Don't you know who* **Jack** *was?"*

Answer: *"I don't know.* **Jack** *was introduced to me in a room in the Hotel Mayflower, and he was very much interested in forming a national veterans' organization and getting out a paper similar to the 'National Tribune,' and he said he had been to see General Butler several times and he was a great friend of his, and I think either Doyle or myself said I would like to meet the general, and that is how the whole thing came up. This fellow said, 'I will call him up and make an appointment.' He said, 'You are going back to New York, and you can stop there to see him.' He called up from the Mayflower Hotel and made an appointment for us to see the general."*

Introduction

On June 26, 2028, Zak Newman, an adventurous 17-year-old, created his first time-travel log entry. He described the miseries of life in America in the year 2028 under the dominion and control of the repressive government known disparagingly as "MOM." As chronicled in *Saving JFK*, he and his friends, twin brother and sister Ethan and Emma Callan-Wright, and inventor Dr. A.C. Currant, first used the *TimeTravelle* time machine to enter the world of 1963 to attempt to save the life of President John F. Kennedy. From Zak's diary:

"I can't say enough bad things about MOM—she has location-revealing nano-implants delivered into the bloodstreams of unsuspecting children when they are immunized against disease; mind-control devices that continuously force-feed mental poison into the masses; monitoring cameras and microphones in every inch of public space; police armed with sound detectors able to listen in on private conversations from a half-kilometer distance; and sensing devices in every police cruiser that can identify every license plate number, every occupant, and anything and everything in a person's vehicle.

MOM is like a nasty, nosy dog with very bad breath—totally invasive, always in your face, everywhere and nowhere, sniffing about without reason—just an annoying pest that will never leave you alone. She always claims to be working in everyone's best interest, offering the comfort of security and protection, but nobody wants her, and nobody likes her—she's just a bitch. I've been told that many years ago, people and politicians actually discussed the limits of MOM. Many suggested that the government's real job is to maintain the free flow of ideas and accomplishments by protecting the people from outsiders or insiders who might interfere with the

'American Dream,' as it was then called.

After a while, MOM poked her snoopy wet nose into everybody's life—according to her, to help 'them' because 'they' could not possibly help themselves. She became nosier and nosier. She kept improving her hunting dog senses and memory until people now believe that she can identify any individual harboring any unwanted thought anywhere on the planet. Even if this is not true, the people are timid and fearful. This long-distance mind-reading could be just a wild rumor, but I notice more people humming to themselves as they walk about in public. Maybe they're trying to stifle their thoughts. After all, if you don't have a thought, it can't be read.

As A.C. Currant, the inventor of the TimeTravelle proclaimed boldly from the safety of his underground bunker, 'Screw MOM!' And I'll second that motion. It's time to do something about her. It's time to fix things."

The time-traveling twins and Zak are now 23 years old. They remain steadfast in improving their world by changing the past. They have returned to the year 2033. Following their time-travel adventures, life has not improved. Their world remains a cocoon of ignorance caught in a web of fear. The skies are full of spying drones—from giant triangular flying platforms to insect-sized bugs. All conversations, human interaction, and even personal thoughts may be monitored, though no one in their hometown of Mystic Heights knows for sure because the reality of the outside world is unknown. Citizens do not speculate. They do not congregate; they do not complain; they do not have opinions. And they never attempt to venture into the unknown. It's too dangerous. People often disappear in the middle of the night. It's a prison world, filled with entertaining government-approved distractions designed to keep the minds of the masses occupied and confused. However, escape is possible for some who have a time machine like Dr. Currant's *TimeTravelle*.

Most people in the future view time travel as science fiction. Zak, Emma, and Ethan know better. It's real.

They've done it. Despite all the risks, including capture by MOM's time-cops, they did it again when they traveled from 2033 to 1933 to Miami, Florida, to save President-elect Franklin Delano Roosevelt from an assassin's bullet. After their mission, the time travelers returned home, back to the future, thinking they had finally fixed history and hoping that the future was a better place.

-Chapter I-

The End

Ground zero, the top of the cliff overlooking Smuggler's Cove, was still smoldering. A nasty wind blew in from the choppy Atlantic below, slid up the cliff wall, and rolled over the top. The splotches of rising gray smoke swirled into the cold, dull autumn sky. A few soldiers wearing yellow hazmat suits cautiously poked through the remains while a tight group of robocops stood on the crater's edge. Little remained of the top of the hill, which had been the site of a memorial park decades ago. The bowl-shaped depression in the center of the rubble was the locus of the massive explosion. Broken stone columns roughly marked the location of the structure that once had capped the hill, appearing like dead trees poking through a swamp of crushed concrete, steel, and rock. Two men wearing camouflage combat fatigues stood at the edge of the destruction, watching the work of the search team.

"We almost had them, sir," shouted the bigger man, his words nearly lost in the wind.

"Almost doesn't count," returned the other. "Lucky for us, we didn't get caught up in this mess. Another five minutes and we would have joined the party. Whoever they were, they took the easy way out. Whether by design or mistake."

"Do you think they knew we were coming?"

The older soldier stood silent for a moment. "If they committed suicide, they would have taken us with them. I'd guess something went wrong. I think this was more than just a hideout for the resistance. Maybe a bomb factory."

"Doesn't look like much...."

"Hard to tell. Given the extent of the damage, anyone down there is dead. But dead men still can talk. I want bodies or body parts. I want to know who they were and what they were doing. Obviously, there was some kind of underground building. Get some equipment up here. Make sure those bots dig this shit out of here very carefully. Don't mess it up. Treat it like a crime scene. It's all evidence."

"Evidence of what?"

"That's your job, Lieutenant. Find out. Dig it out. I.D. it. Analyze it. Preserve it. And get a thorough report from our lab people that makes sense of this whole thing. If you find bodies, pieces, or anything else of interest, send me photos and get it to the lab immediately."

For a moment, they surveyed the smoldering blast site. Scattered plumes of smoke rose from the jumbled surface like dancing ghosts. A bird circled high above.

"Still there," said the Lieutenant squinting as he looked.

"What?"

"Maybe a pigeon, sir." He pointed to the speck in the sky. "That little bastard is determined."

As the older man walked away, he turned and shouted, "The bird might be evidence. Shoot it down if you can."

-Chapter II-

A New Assignment

Jack Travers sat on the passenger side. The Secret Service agent behind the wheel didn't even attempt to converse. That was fine with Jack. He preferred solitude to small talk. He welcomed the warmth of the early morning sun intermittently striking his face as it flickered through the tree branches above. His elbow jutted out the open window of the 1932 Chevrolet. He angled his head toward the window, allowing the wind to rustle his hair. He was enjoying this brief excursion through the Hudson River Valley. The land was alive with the green growth of early summer. Flocks of hungry birds dropped down onto the open fields to feed and returned skyward, heading toward the shade and peace of the surrounding woods. Nature ignored the chaotic world of humanity, the world of economic depression and political turmoil. For the moment, Jack resolved to do the same. With some pleasure, he lit a cigarette, took a deep drag, leaned his head back, and exhaled the smoke.

As the Secret Service agent skillfully handled the winding road leading to Val-Kill, Jack recalled his previous trip to Mrs. Roosevelt's private retreat last February. She had been distressed, knowing her husband might die in Miami. She had given Jack the task of assuring that Franklin Roosevelt did not become collateral damage from the impending mob hit on the Mayor of Chicago. Safeguarding FDR was Travers' last major assignment from Eleanor Roosevelt. Fortunately, he completed his job successfully. The gun aimed at the President's head never fired. Working for Jack, time traveler A.C. Currant altered history and saved Franklin Roosevelt by taking out the second gunman before he shot at FDR.

A different gun, fired by a mob hitman patsy, a

motivated Italian immigrant named Zangara, had found its target, killing Mayor Anton Cermak. Now Zangara was dead. Ethan Callan-Wright's newfound girlfriend was also killed, and Ethan's twin sister Emma, the love of Jack's life, had gone back home. Jack wondered if she would return. She had promised that she would come back to him. He closed his eyes. An image of Emma's face appeared for a second, smiling, and her bright green eyes were dancing. For a few moments, he soaked in her memory. Then slowly, he opened his eyes, saving himself from the pain of her absence.

The car negotiated a smooth curve, and a simple gray stone cottage appeared in the distance. Its rustic reflection rested peacefully on the surface of a small pond separated from its source by a line of waving cattails hugging the grassy hillside shore. They approached the cottage entrance, and memories flooded Jack's mind. Four months and five days had passed since that crazy night of the assassins, February 15, 1933. A few weeks later, Franklin Roosevelt, the 32nd President of the United States, was inaugurated, and Eleanor Roosevelt became America's First Lady. Jack Travers' attention returned to the present as the car slid to a stop crunching on pebbles. The agent killed the engine and set the handbrake. Then, all was quiet.

The driver turned to face him, wearing the usual grim face of his breed. "Wait here, please, Mr. Travers," he said. The man left the car, entered the house, and returned quickly. "She'll be with you in a moment. She asked that you wait. Follow me."

Travers followed the agent to the front door of the modest building. Another agent, inside the doorway, escorted him to an area located off the living room in what might be called a book nook: two windows at the corner, floor-to-ceiling bookshelves, two wing chairs, and a little round table wearing an embroidered white tablecloth. Jack sat in the chair facing the door, waiting. The agent padded out of the house on cat feet.

The morning was warming. Open windows gathered

country smells carried in by soft breezes that gently nudged the lacy white curtains. A serving set had been placed on the table along with iced lemonade in a translucent green glass pitcher glowing in a beam of sunlight. Jack focused on the dripping beads of condensation slowly seeping into the tablecloth below. His eyes wandered. Light-wood paneling, overstuffed furniture, walls covered in bric-a-brac, and overhead wood beams created an almost too-cozy space. But he knew that Mrs. Roosevelt treasured the humble little setting in the woods as her own. It was her place and how she lived within it was her choice. Val-Kill offered her peace and solitude. It was a retreat away from the big house, away from her mother-in-law, reporters, smoke-filled rooms, and the rigorous schedule of White House life. It was even an escape from her husband.

On the fireplace mantle, the clock ticked. The incessant mechanical metronomic sound filled the quiet room. Jack had an ear for the sound of timepieces. Inevitably, they focused his attention on the concept of time as a constant reminder of the transitory nature of his life. He glanced at his wristwatch and then checked one timekeeper against the other. They disagreed by minutes. The anomaly gnawed at him. He looked out the window, and in the distance, he spotted a familiar figure approaching. She entered the attached porch. Seconds later, the door to the main house opened. His employer looked very comfortable. She wore a short-sleeved yellow sundress, matching bandana, and white tennis shoes and carried a wrapping of cut flowers. Always surprised by the physical presence of this very tall woman who filled much of the tiny space upon entering, Jack stood up quickly. "Hello, Mrs. Roosevelt. I'm here," he sputtered.

She chuckled. "Yes, Jack. I can see that." A big toothy smile filled her face. "Please sit down. I'll return shortly." She left his line of vision and returned in a moment to shake hands and sit in the chair opposite Jack. Taking a handkerchief from her dress pocket, she dabbed her forehead gently. "The heat is coming up early today.

Would you do the honors?"

He thought about it for a moment. "Certainly." He poured two glasses of juice and made an assumption; he carefully placed them on the little round doilies that looked too fancy to be coasters.

"Thank you, Jack." She sipped the lemonade. "And thank you for coming. How is that fine lady Emma? Feeling better, I hope." She smiled. Her large blue eyes revealed an honest inquiry.

"Yes, she is. I just received a letter from her. She's recovering nicely from that return bout of TB. She hopes to get back to Washington soon."

Mrs. Roosevelt set down her glass and straightened up in her chair. "I hope so. I miss that girl."

Jack nodded and smiled. He leaned back slightly in his chair and exhaled. "How is the President?"

She laughed lightly. "Franklin is fit as a fiddle. He loves the action. He's in the arena now, Jack. And there's nothing he enjoys more than that." She paused. "Thanks to you, I might add. I know we've talked about this, but I want to thank you again for your work in Miami. You did a fine job. I'm sorry about the mayor. May he rest in peace. But life goes on...."

Jack picked up the dangle in the conversation. "That was a close call." He had never mentioned that her husband was the target of another shooter. It was best that she and, he supposed, FDR believed that Mayor Cermak was the only intended victim that night. Their conversation stopped for a moment. They sipped their lemonades as if there was little else to say about all the dark characters lurking in the corners of life, waiting for an opportunity to use violence to solve problems.

She held her hands together in her lap. Her eyes said she was formulating an approach. Jack was familiar with this. She was a very thoughtful person, very concise and deliberate. "I need your help again, Jack. Thankfully this has nothing to do with the jackals in Chicago, but we have our share of people in Washington and New York seeking to control events and the people of America." She smiled at him. "This is going to take a while," she said quietly. "Why don't you remove your jacket? Get comfortable. We have plenty to cover."

"All right." He stood and removed his suit jacket, folded it, placed it on a nearby chair, and seated himself.

"First, let me give you an overview." She paused. "Some of this you may know. But I want you to get my perspective."

"Of course."

She continued. "Franklin won the election by a landslide. However, some are not pleased to have him in office. A group of powerful people is afraid of the current economic situation and concerned that they will not be able to maintain the status quo. They suspect he may lean to the left and lead this country into socialism or, worse yet...communism. Others think he intends to become a dictator, commandeering every available young man and requiring them to swear allegiance to him." She took a deep breath and shook her head gently. "Like a Mussolini or a Hitler."

"That's ridiculous," said Jack.

"You and I know that, but they're also people in the country, without power, who are suffering. Common people, you might say, who would welcome a strongman. Someone who would promise them a stable, predictable, reliable future. And others have the power and want to keep it. They would like someone whom they control. Everyone is looking for someone who can grab the reins of power and end our economic woes. The concept of fascism is attractive to them." She sighed. "These are challenging times. We are in danger of losing the Republic, Jack." Her voice rose in pitch with this pronouncement.

Jack sensed her concern, but he had never mentally coupled Franklin Roosevelt with Adolph Hitler. From what he knew, this was a bizarre comparison. "The people were looking for a strong leader," he said. "Someone with new ideas. They have that man in FDR. But he's not a dictator." As he spoke, he listened to his words;

unfortunately, his confident, unemotional, baritone voice sounded almost patronizing.

She visibly tightened upon hearing his comment and paused again before speaking. Her eyes locked on his. "Technically, I am afraid you are wrong, Jack. The President is a dictator. It is something he created on purpose. His desire is to have that power...only employed for the good of the people. And to allow him to remain in power."

"Sorry, Mrs. Roosevelt, I'm not following you."

She relaxed, and her voice calmed. "Most people are not following Franklin's moves. He is a great politician, and in a way, he is like a magician. As he performs a trick, he has his audience looking elsewhere.

Jack put his elbows on the table and leaned in. "But, what's the trick?" He looked directly into her eyes, seeking an understanding that had eluded him.

"Of course, you listened to his inauguration speech," she said.

He nodded. "It was a great speech."

"It was," she affirmed. "Franklin focused everyone's attention on the fact that the banks were failing and that current economic conditions had created a 'state of emergency.' Like in wartime. In this case, the country is in a war against the bankers, poverty, joblessness, and, of course, 'fear itself.' His response to this attack on our economy was to declare a 'bank holiday'". She smiled. "Who could resist a holiday from all the financial problems which faced the nation?"

Jack nodded. "Right. The banks closed for a few days. Their solvencies were evaluated. And then they reopened. People believed something positive was happening, and their confidence in the monetary system returned. They re-deposited their 'mattress' money into the banking system. It was brilliant."

"Yes. But people did not focus on his declaration of an official 'state of emergency' ratified by Congress a few days later. At that point, all the acts and proclamations of the President become the law of the land. Legally, Franklin, at that moment, gave himself the same level of power held by Hitler and Mussolini. After that, he could seize and purchase all the gold in the country. And inflate the amount of money in circulation. He is, by all accounts, a dictator."

Jack leaned back in his chair. He knew something about FDR's first few decisive months in office. The public believed the new President separated himself from the actions of his predecessor Herbert Hoover. But Jack also knew that some of the recent economic programs of the first hundred days after the inauguration didn't appear out of thin air. Many of these were programs that President Hoover's advisors had developed. Of course, FDR took action; Hoover did not. However, Jack was only subconsciously aware of the implications of the 'state of emergency.' These thoughts swirled in his head as he struggled to deal with this blind spot in his thinking. "I just don't see the President as a dictator," he sputtered.

"Certainly, I agree," she said, sounding almost indignant, "but he is a man who is taking every precaution. The people did elect him, and he wanted to serve. Unfortunately, many do not wish him well, Jack." She sipped from her lemonade and seemed to gather her thoughts. "The power of an American president is usually held in check by the bond between him and the people. He will not be reelected if he deviates too far from their expectations. He may even face impeachment if serious problems arise."

Jack saw where she was heading. "But with this decision to declare a national emergency, the President immediately settled most of the questions about the extent of his power. He is the boss and the Commander-in-Chief of the military. This point was well-made in his radio speech to the American Legion members just a few days after taking office. Maybe a million or so former soldiers. Men who took an oath of allegiance to the Commander. I assume he wanted them to know that he was the boss. I know he changed the tone of his speech to sound less imperious, but he still made his point." He paused. "Are you saying there is a possibility of a *putsch*?"

She nodded. "That's a good choice of words given the recent events in Germany. Ten years ago, Hitler attempted a military *coup* backed up by his private army. It failed, but he learned a lesson. He decided to work within the system. This year he became chancellor. Once in power, a law was passed that effectively gave him total control of the country."

Jack shrugged his shoulders. "From what you've just said, Mr. Roosevelt may have assumed a similar position."

She frowned and shook her head gently. "Like you, I don't like any comparisons with that man in Germany. The President has the power, but the people of the United States are not fanatical. They may respect Franklin. They may even love him. Some may see him as a savior. Nevertheless, I believe they have retained their critical judgment. The President's only interest is to preserve our system of government, not to destroy it. And the people sense that."

Jack lowered his eyes. "It is a fine line," he said quietly.

She smiled. "The President is very skilled in the art of walking the political tightrope. At the moment, thankfully, he has the support of the people, the Congress, the Supreme Court, the newspapers, and even to some degree, the support of his potential enemies."

"Who are they?"

"There are many big cats out there waiting to pounce: populists like Huey Long, leaders of fascist groups, and recalcitrant industrialists like Henry Ford. The most dangerous are the bankers. For the moment, the President has them in check. He's saved their banks, but he's also raised the price of gold, creating more money for him to spend. This increases his power. The bankers appear to be playing his game for now, but they are positioning themselves."

Jack rubbed his chin. "So...you fear they may be working behind the scenes to grab power?"

She was about to answer, but then she moved her chair back and rose. "Jack, let's take a little walk in the woods."

He stood as she continued. "We need to overturn the conspiracy. Make it visible. You know how the bugs that cling to a rock's underside always scurry away when exposed to the light of the day. That's what bugs and other such creatures do. That's what needs to be done."

Jack followed her out of the cottage, and a short walk brought them to a meandering path. As they strolled, the sun filtered through the leafy canopy above while a light breeze stirred the air. He glanced at her. She walked with strength. He knew she was determined to support her husband.

She looked at him. "I love it here, Jack. It's so beautiful and quiet in the woods."

He nodded and looked over his shoulder. Behind them, out of earshot, a Secret Service agent followed. His presence reminded Jack of the dangers of being a politician. Someone was always gunning for your job. He didn't envy Franklin Roosevelt. He was a man who had overcome his severe physical limitations to grab the Presidential brass ring, but he was a soft target. The news media followed the unwritten rule of never printing photos of him that would expose his physical weakness. Unable to walk and confined to a wheelchair, he was an easy target for negative propaganda or even a physical attack. His power hinged on maintaining a psychological edge. He had to have the people and the news reporters supporting him. He also had to keep his political and governmental power. He spun a delicate web of charm, bluster, and physical ability.

Jack knew the physical power of the President under the worst circumstances might boil down to the number of troops under his command. The numbers were not impressively positive for the President. As Commander-in-Chief, he controlled about 165,000 soldiers under General Douglas MacArthur's direction. Some of these troops had been ordered by MacArthur to attack the Bonus Marchers in 1932. Jack knew the General was a man who made FDR nervous—someone to keep very close or far away.

A few days ago, 200,000 National Guard troops in all the states were subjected to a new law requiring them to take direction from FDR as their Commander in the event of a national emergency. Roosevelt could count on their support because the banking crisis had been declared an emergency. Finally, one of FDR's first acts as President was to create the Civilian Conservation Corps. This program proved very popular with the public. Already over 250,000 young men had been conscripted. They were trained by the War Department and given uniforms. These 'peaceable soldiers' planted trees, built small roads and bridges, and fought fires in national and state forest areas. For this, they received thirty dollars per month. Roosevelt had also issued an Executive Order to permit veterans to join the tree-planting program. With this program, FDR corralled the out-of-work youth of America and co-opted thousands of potential dissidents. Moreover, if push came to shove, the C.C.C. boys could be trained and armed. In total, FDR had the potential of about 600,000 men who might back him against a *coup* attempt.

On the other side, disenfranchised, disillusioned, well-trained war veterans, some battle-hardened members of the American Legion and the Veterans of Foreign Wars numbered more than one million men, and they remained wildcard players in any potential *putsch*. History had shown the importance of such men in the Nazi takeover of Germany. Travers had done his homework, and nothing Mrs. Roosevelt had told him was news, except for her suggesting her husband was a dictator.

They continued along the path. "Well, back to business." She quietly cleared her throat. "I'll get to you now and your new assignment. I have information that some wealthy and powerful people, maybe even some within the President's Brains Trust and inner-circle, are making plans to push the President aside and create an alternate form of government here in America."

"By force?" he asked.

"That's probably their last resort. These men would rather make the whole process smooth, seamless, and almost undetectable by the American people. But I have been told they are working to create a military force that they can use to back up their will if necessary. Part of their plan is already in place. They have attempted to establish another leader to replace Franklin."

Above, a startled flock of crows abandoned the treetops in a noisy rush causing the couple to stop and look up.

He turned back to face her. "Did this person appear on the cover of *Time* magazine as the 'Man of the Year?'"

"Very perceptive, Jack. That's correct. General Hugh Johnson appears to be the man waiting in the wings. He is part of their plan. They'll do some political gerrymandering to move Johnson up, along with slandering and deriding Franklin. They'll try to arrange it so that either the President will be forced to resign or they will neuter him."

"But...you said the President had dictatorial powers."

She sighed. "In theory. But no one wants to start a civil war. What I'm asking of you, Jack is simple. I want you to derail their plans. We know they want to assemble a unified political faction of war vets. They are relying on the American Legion veterans to back them. You know the leader of that group has promoted fascism. Ten years ago, he proclaimed Mussolini and fascism as a positive model for America, and some of their members became strikebreakers. But the Legion has been losing members to the Veterans of Foreign Wars group."

Jack interrupted. "I'm familiar with General Butler and the V.F.W. I listened to him at the Bonus March in Anacostia in '32."

She rolled her eyes. "General Butler is a patriot but not a politician. His goals are at odds with the President's policies. There is just not enough money to go around. The veterans' benefits are currently one-quarter of the entire federal budget. The government certainly cannot afford to pay the bonus that General Butler and the V.F.W. wants. They're all good, patriotic people, Jack.

But, as you know, the President created the Economy Act earlier this year which took away some veteran benefits. And he created the Civilian Conservation Corps, which caused another uproar among the V.F.W. people. They see him as abandoning the soldiers in favor of young men who don't have families and responsibilities. The point is the V.F.W. is ripe to be gathered into the sphere of the plotters."

"What can I do?" he asked.

She looked away from him across the open fields. "You can become a defector." She said the words quietly, and then turned to face him again. "Present yourself as someone who disagrees with the President's policies. Give them the appearance that you will work with them under cover. Find out who is in charge of the attempt to co-opt the V.F.W, and fix it, so their plans fail."

Jack thought for a moment. "If I'm found out, I'll be viewed as a traitor to the President and the country."

Mrs. Roosevelt moved closer to him and held both his shoulders tightly. Their faces only a foot apart, her moist eyes revealed her concern. "Do it for me, Jack." She swallowed. "It is an important and necessary task."

Jack nodded. "I will."

Seconds passed, and she released her grip and gently took his arm. The forest grew quiet as they headed back to the cottage, hurrying now as the sky had darkened and the wind was building. A storm was approaching.

O.A. LOG   TTA2033-5
INVESTIGATOR: Jack Travers
DATE: June 12, 1933
PROJECT: FDR
PROGRESS REPORT: I continue to act in my role as special assistant to ELEANOR ROOSEVELT.
Meeting with ELEANOR ROOSEVELT — Two days ago, I met with Mrs. ROOSEVELT at her request at her country estate. She expressed concern that there are fascist forces that are seeking to either remove FRANKLIN ROOSEVELT from the Office of President or leave him in place, but eliminate him as an effective leader. She identified GENERAL HUGH JOHNSON as a person within the current administration who may be involved in a plot against the President. JOHNSON heads the National Recovery Administration, a newly formed agency established to control prices, wages, and production and employment practices. She did not explain her reasons for her concern about JOHNSON. We know he was responsible for implementing a program of the conscription of citizen soldiers in the World War. His war record reflects a man of determination and willingness to do whatever is necessary to move the agenda of his superiors forward, even if it requires him to work outside the law. For his successful efforts in the drafting of men in the years 1916/1917, he was promoted from Captain to Brigadier General in 1918. Later he worked with the War Industries Board and became acquainted with many influential businessmen. Mrs. ROOSEVELT appears to have identified him as a possible threat to the Roosevelt presidency.
Also, Mrs. ROOSEVELT is concerned that if armed forces became involved in any takeover attempt, these could include the members of veterans' groups, specifically the World War veterans. She has directed me to stop the establishment of a coalition of the American Legion and Veterans of Foreign Wars organizations. I will become involved in this project, working to ensure a favorable result in conformance with *The History*.

TRANSMITTED VIA CODED TIME JUSTIFIER 16:09 ET

.

-Chapter III-

Not Again

Standing at one end of the conference table, Jacques DuFour struck a pose familiar to Ethan. In a Proustian flash of recognition, Ethan's mind slipped back to his high school history class. *M. DuFour* was in his element. He spoke in a gentle voice tinged with a French accent. He was again *Le Professeur*. He had all the facts, names, dates, biographies, and props, which made his fascinating tale of 1934, at once, both unbelievable yet credible. Ethan squirmed in his chair as he listened to DuFour's slow, deliberate presentation. He made throat-clearing noises. The others at the table eyeballed him, but DuFour continued, lost in his work. Having captured the attention of those gathered, Warren Wright, Emma, Ethan, Dr. A.C. Currant, and Zak Newman, DuFour would not easily relinquish the platform.

Bursting with a mixture of anger and disappointment, Ethan stood abruptly. He was big and tall, and his physical presence always made a statement. While comfortably spacious, his father's private office became noticeably cramped as Ethan's six-foot-five-inch frame towered over those seated. He overwhelmed his diminutive former history teacher. Somewhat stunned, DuFour stood toe-to-toe with Ethan. Slowly he inquired, "Ethan. Do you have something you wish to express?"

"I can't believe this. This is just like last time. We go there. We fix things. And what happens? And FDR is out again. This is crazy!"

"Ethan. Sit down. You're making the Professor nervous. It's not his fault," said Emma.

Ethan looked down at his former teacher. "Sorry, Mr. DuFour. I'm just...." With that, he sat. He put his elbows on the table and held his head in his hands.

"I'm with you, Ethan," said A.C. Currant, "we worked

hard to save old FDR. Too hard to have him run out of office in his first year as President. But let's have DuFour give us the news. We can only play the cards in our hands. Let's see what we're holding."

DuFour remained standing. He had a pile of research papers in front of him, awaiting his explanation. "*Merci*, A.C.," he said with a hint of a smile. "Now, let's go back to 1933. Miraculously...Franklin Roosevelt was not assassinated in Miami, Florida, on February 15th. Mr. Cermak was not so lucky, but you people did your job. You did save FDR from death. He was inaugurated as the thirty-second President of the United States on March 4, 1933. John Nance Garner, his running mate, became the Vice President." DuFour reached for a paper and tossed a single sheet onto the table. "*Time* magazine. Very popular in those days. Every year someone would grace its cover as the Man of the Year. As you can see, in 1933, Franklin Roosevelt had the honor."

Zak Newman reached over and picked up the color facsimile image. "That's our boy. FDR. He's looking good." The picture showed a handsome middle-aged man in a blue pin-striped suit with a gold medal pinned to his chest. "Maybe a bit nervous looking."

"You'd be nervous too if you were just handed the government of the United States back in the Great Depression. Tough job," said Warren Wright.

"He looks a bit like you, Dad," said Emma smiling at Warren Wright.

"Not. Maybe Dad's dad," countered Ethan, who had perked up once he saw the image of Roosevelt. "We saved his butt in Miami. If it weren't for A.C., he could have applied for permanent early retirement."

"Ethan, you're so crude. He was...is...a great man," said Emma.

Ethan nodded. "I hope so. I certainly hope so...."

"Go ahead, Jacques," A.C. Currant prodded. "What happened after the inauguration? We left 1933 just a few days before that happened."

"Just to give you an idea of the life and times of 1933,

here's a copy of that same *Time* magazine two months after the FDR Man of the Year issue." DuFour placed another cover facsimile on the table. "Recognize this person?"

"Looks like Adolph Hitler," said Emma.

"Correct. Right at the same time, FDR became President, Hitler became Chancellor of Germany. These were astounding moments. The question could be asked: do these leaders just appear out of nowhere? Or are they developed and supported by rich and powerful forces and then moved into position? Both Hitler and FDR had been visible and active politicians. FDR came from old money. He was positioned for power at birth. A patrician. He married President Theodore Roosevelt's niece. He ran for Vice-President in 1920. He was elected Governor of New York in 1928, and thanks to you and the support of the American people, he became President in 1933.

Mr. Hitler took a different path. He was a penniless commoner and wounded veteran of the World War. In 1923, he was imprisoned for attempting to take control of the country forcibly. He bullied his way into power. By 1932 he had a personal Nazi army of over 400,000 men permitting him to claw and beat his way to the top."

Jacques DuFour placed a copy of the 1934 *Time* magazine featuring the Man of the Year on the table. "Another *Time* cover. About a year later. This gentleman is General Hugh Johnson. FDR brought him in to run the National Recovery Administration. The NRA, as it was called, was put into place to set prices and wages. I think the real goal was to raise them. The intent was to control all businesses nationwide, from the smallest tailor shop to the biggest industrial fabricators. Johnson was a former general in the army during the World War. He organized the conscription of American manpower. It was called the 'draft.' And he worked on a board of price controllers during the war to minimize war profiteering and maximize the industrial war effort. He was a good friend of the financier Bernard Baruch who was instrumental in placing Johnson in power.

Johnson was rough and tough. A hard-drinking, dominating leader. After FDR's fall, he attracted populist support. His physical hyperactivity contrasted with FDR's more restricted lifestyle. They were both charismatic and take-charge leaders. Johnson was sometimes crude and rude but effective. FDR was always a smooth and very effective politician."

Zak flipped through pages of the magazine and then interrupted DuFour. "Hey. The symbol of this NRA thing is a blue eagle. It looks just like the Nazi eagle. What's with all the eagles?"

DuFour smiled. "Yes, Zak. This is true. We had our eagle symbols, and others had theirs. Incidentally, the Blue Eagle could be seen in the show windows of every store, factory, and office building across the country. It symbolized a national patriotic effort to overcome the Great Depression."

Current smiled. "Was it successful?"

"Initially, it was not. But it was a catalyst for General Johnson's rise to power. He was a bullying dynamo who rushed about the country selling the NRA concept and enlisting others to join. He had the entire country in a frenzy about price and wage controls. In fact, this same kind of economic policy had a track record. It was enacted in Nazi Germany by Hitler in the 1930s, and it was very successful in reactivating their economy. As I mentioned, initially, it was a bureaucratic nightmare. Yet, after President Roosevelt's fall from power, Johnson refined the machinery of the NRA and made it a great success, and legal, in the eyes of the Supreme Court."

"What's this about the 'fall' of FDR?" asked Warren Wright.

DuFour looked up, then back at Wright. "This, unfortunately, is the big event that changed history and undermined your valiant efforts." He shrugged his shoulders gently. "You see. Your intervention permitted him to get into power. And he was a very effective leader in his first year. Initially, he was faced with bank failures. States across the nation had declared statewide bank closures. Just a few hours before his inauguration, New York and Illinois closed all their banks. After his famous 'the only thing we have to fear is fear itself' speech, he closed down all the banks in the country. In the first of his coast-to-coast radio 'fireside' chats, he called it a 'bank holiday.' His melodious voice made this concept sound like a trip to the seashore. Immediately after, no citizen could deposit or remove money from their bank accounts for a short while. Thousands of banks had failed nationwide. But this 'bank holiday' stopped the run."

"Did this work? Mr. DuFour. Or did people complain and riot? This was a crazy period in American history," said Emma.

DuFour nodded gently. "But, yes. To say the least. However, Roosevelt's quick action worked. There were no riots. After several days of evaluation as to which banks should re-open and which should remain shuttered, the holiday was over. The public's fear subsided. FDR had saved the day. The hoarders removed their money from under the mattress and returned it to the banks."

"So, FDR was leading the country out of the depression," said Emma.

"He was. This was his 'New Deal,' as he called it. At this point, he had declared the country to be in a state of emergency, and he had almost absolute power. His next move was to call in all the country's gold. You might think this would have stirred up the populace. But it didn't. FDR demanded that everyone who owned gold money turn it into the government in exchange for newly printed Federal Reserve Notes. There were severe penalties for anyone not complying."

"What's the point of this?" asked A.C. Currant. "Those gold coins were valuable."

"That is correct, A.C., But FDR wanted to build the United States Treasury. Once the government had all the gold in the country, he raised the official price of gold from about twenty dollars per ounce to thirty-five dollars. Thus, he increased the amount of money available for his government projects by devaluing the dollar by about forty percent. It gave him more power."

"Seems like an instant tax on the entire population," said Currant.

"That it was."

"What projects?" asked Zak.

"Many. Like the Civilian Conservation Corps, which took hundreds of thousands of young unemployed men out of the cities and relocated them to camps in the rural areas where they would plant trees and build roads and park structures. The W.P.A. or Works Progress Administration was another program to employ the unemployed by giving them construction jobs on public improvements."

"So instead of strengthening private business to create jobs, he just created jobs out of thin air with an artificially inflated Federal bank account," said Currant.

"You might say that. But Roosevelt intended to do both. Build the private sector and give people jobs. Get the country going again. Restore confidence. And all of this helped. And he repealed the Prohibition Act, which allowed liquor to be sold and distributed. This was very popular."

"Aside from freeing the booze, it seems somewhat socialistic," suggested Currant.

"Some at the time thought so. Many people disapproved of this government interference. They preferred to let the capitalist system fix itself. I imagine the rich and powerful were unhappy with Roosevelt's aggressive approach."

Ethan frowned. "I don't get it. Seems like everything he did could help the economy. The people didn't object to his methods. What's the problem? Why the fall?"

DuFour rubbed his hands together and looked around the table. They were all anticipating his answer. "Yes. Yes." He shook his head gently. "It seems improbable. But the fall I am speaking of has a dual meaning." He paused. "FDR fell...and then he fell from power. Very strange indeed. A little more history." He looked at Ethan. "You were in Miami. You saw the man. He was in a wheelchair.

Right?"

"Right," said Ethan.

"Because of a disease which struck him in 1921, he could not use his lower body. His legs were useless for balance or locomotion. Oh, yes, he adapted quite well to his unfortunate situation. He learned how to do a kind of 'walk' well enough to convince most Americans that he was not handicapped. Remember, in those days, the president was not so much seen as he was heard. Radio was the communications medium of the day, and he had an excellent radio voice. Although he was a commanding presence in person with a bold personality, his public appearances never featured him in his wheelchair. And his ability to simulate walking for short distances gave him an appearance of normality. You might say the people of America believed what they chose to believe. They saw a strong man and a strong leader whom they had elected to lift them out of the Great Depression. That was the image Roosevelt had to maintain. Therefore, the news media did not show photos of him in the wheelchair. They did not talk about his physical limitations. He was always seen sitting behind a desk, in his car, piloting a sailboat, standing at a lectern, or engaging in water polo".

"The deception worked until April 24, 1934. That day FDR visited Griffith Stadium in Washington, D.C., for a Washington Senators baseball game against the Boston Red Sox. As usual, he wore special leg braces, which allowed him to lock his legs straight. With these braces, he could simulate walking by swinging his legs forward one at a time and shifting his weight over the landing leg while holding on to the arm of his powerfully built son. It was more a waddle than a walk, but the braces allowed him to stand."

"On the opening day of the baseball season, before the game started, he held a baseball in throwing position, ready to toss out the first pitch. This was an outstanding photo opportunity and allowed thousands of fans at the game to see their President in action. They cheered loudly as he momentarily held the ball. Smiling broadly, wearing his fedora and business suit, he had the ball high in his right hand and braced with his left hand on the low wall in front of him. At that moment, he looked as solid as bedrock. He tossed the ball into the mitt of the Senators' catcher. The newsreel and *Speed Graphic* cameras recorded this history."

"But then something happened. As viewed by thousands of fans at the game and later millions of people via newsreel images, he fell. It appeared as if the left leg had collapsed. For part of a second, he balanced on one leg. Then he tipped over like a stone statue dropping to his right, arms out-stretched to break his fall, crashing viciously into the lap of a seated man. Then he disappeared from view, behind the bunting covering the pipe railings."

"Astounded dignitaries in the area, including at least one baseball player and Secret Service agents, rushed to retrieve the President. It was a chaotic rescue. Too many people in one place. There was an audible tone of concern from the crowd. Some men attempting to help ended up stepping on Roosevelt. Others were knocked onto the playing field by bodyguards. The crowd watched in shock. It took at least a minute to pull the President up and raise him into a standing position. He appeared disheveled and dazed as he was held upright by men at either side. His hat was gone. Some chewing gum lodged in his hair. The right side of his forehead was cut and bleeding profusely. In the confined space of the box seat, those attempting to move his body strained. He faced the wrong direction. Slowly three men rudely reversed the direction of his rigid body. And then they dragged him out of sight into an area below the stands. It was all very frightening and disturbing. I will show you."

DuFour activated a nearby vision screen, and a black and white movie played to the small audience in Wright's office. The clip ran a couple of minutes, and by its completion, Emma was crying. Her brother Ethan offered her a tissue.

A.C. Currant rolled his eyes and spoke. "That was it

for FDR, right?"

DuFour opened his hands in a gesture of defeat. "FDR's people tried to put the proverbial cat back in the bag, but his image was crushed, and the nationwide outcry was unstoppable. The people of America saw that their concept of the President was unrealistic. They saw a man who could not stand on his own. A man who could not rescue himself. A man who was too weak and frail to be their leader."

"While most felt pity and many still approved of him as a person, the deception was obvious. Everyone in the White House quickly tried to make sense of this tragedy and repair the damage. The Democratic Party leaders met with the President in closed-door sessions. The result was a compromise. FDR would remain, but General Hugh Johnson, a powerful, virile, active, healthy man, would take over the day-to-day responsibilities of executive government and become the new face of the White House."

"What happened to FDR?" asked Emma, still sniffling.

DuFour thought before speaking. "He was humiliated by the fall, his apparent weakness, and the national outrage and disappointment expressed at movie theaters across the country. FDR was, after that, a broken Humpty Dumpty. He drifted into the background. He drank too much. He sought comfort from his close friends. He went fishing often. He seemed to lose his magical political powers. The boisterous Hugh Johnson took his place in the public eye. Even FDR's fireside chats no longer carried the airwaves as before. The public turned a deaf ear to his dramatic speeches. They preferred the gruff utterances of the former Army general to the voice of the man who had deceived them so blatantly."

"Why did he fall? What the heck happened that day?" asked Zak.

"No one knows for sure. But it was an equipment failure," answered DuFour. "Curiously, the locks on both leg braces failed almost simultaneously."

"Was there any investigation?"

"I'm sure there was a private investigation by the FDR team, but no particular explanation was cited. In the end, it was viewed as just bad luck," answered DuFour.

"Did FDR run again?" asked Ethan.

"No. His term of office ended in 1936. FDR, Vice-President Gardner, and Secretary of General Affairs Hugh Johnson left the White House. The Republican candidate won the next election. The economy had improved dramatically after FDR's fall. His job programs dissipated, the gold standard was affirmed, the state of national emergency was rescinded, and following the 1936 election, history proceeded much in the way we understand it to be."

The room went quiet. Then Zak spoke. "That's very interesting. But we know what happens a hundred years later. Nothing has changed. We end up where we are...living our lives in a fancy prison society with MOM as the warden. What happened to the land of the free and the home of the brave? We have to do something."

Warren Wright glanced at his daughter and son, looking concerned. "Zak, I was hoping you guys would give it up. Stay home. Enjoy our imperfect but relatively comfortable life."

"Sorry, Mr. Wright," said Zak. "But it's all a lie. We know that, and you know that. We can't live like this."

"Zak's right, Dad," said Emma. "It's like that old movie, *The Truman Show.* 'Good morning, good afternoon, and good evening.' Every day is perfect—if you're oblivious to the truth. Humanity's children were adopted by corporations. We only know part of the truth of our world. Thanks to A.C.'s machine, we know more. The rest of our supposed understanding is propaganda. *The History* is the bible. MOM is the Pope. And patriotism is our religion."

Ethan jumped in. "Do you know if FDR's braces ever failed him before?"

DuFour thought for a moment. He rubbed his koala bear beard. "No," he said, shaking his head, "there is no mention of a previous failure."

"*Hijole!* That's it." Zak smiled and nodded.

"That's what?" asked Emma.

"That's what happened to our boy FDR," Zak said excitedly. "Someone messed with his braces. Someone who wanted to assassinate him politically. Someone wanted him out of the way. It was perfect. No blood. No shooters. No poison. Very clean. Set up a strong boss in his midst. Make Roosevelt look feeble and incompetent. Then manipulate public opinion and take over."

"You've got it, Zak. We're back in business!" exclaimed Ethan. He looked at the others and smiled smugly. "One more trip, gang. We'll get ahead of this folding-leg plot. And we'll make sure the gangsters behind it are neutralized. And Franklin D. Roosevelt will continue as President of the United States of America."

The renegade group had held their meeting in Warren Wright's inner sanctum, his secure office, a room that had been cleverly designed to foil MOM's surveillance. The office was cloaked physically and electronically so that it was not visible to her various electronic sensors. Even MOM's latest bio-photonic sensors were excluded. The meeting ended, and they left the house in pairs, with staggered departures. Zak and Ethan had hopped a drone cab to town. And the two bachelors, Currant and DuFour decided to go bowling. Emma knew it was the one thing they had in common. Both men loved the game. DuFour had few interests outside history; Currant had many interests, but history was not one of them. But they were both avid bowlers.

Emma and her father decided to go for an early evening walk. She had something to discuss. It was somewhat safer to converse in the open air. At least, this was a common belief. They knew the drones were active somewhere in the sky above. They couldn't see them. Some were designed to appear bat-like; others like hawks that floated on the thermals. Emma looked up. The sky looked clear except for a noisy flock of geese heading north. Father and daughter walked briskly. The waning sun played peek-a-boo through the branches of the massive oak trees lining the sidewalk. It was late March, still the cold season for Mystic Heights. The weather was crisp, dry, and windless. For a while, they walked without speaking. She sensed that her father did not want to discuss the obvious, but she knew she must. Like everyone else who valued their privacy in MOM's world, they talked in the code of obscurity and generalities.

"Nice night for a walk, Dad," she opened.

"That it is." Warren Wright nodded as he spoke.

"It looks like we'll be taking one more trip."

"I guess there is no stopping you."

"Nor Ethan. He won't quit."

"How can you be certain it's worth it, Emma? You can't predict the future. Maybe if you're lucky, you can choose people, but after that...". Warren Wright's voice trailed off, and he gazed up. He took a deep breath. "You know, I worry about you, Emma. I worry about all of you."

"Even A.C.?" She smiled.

"Yes." He scoffed.

She took a deep breath. "This will be my last visit. I'm staying this time."

He said nothing and fixed his gaze ahead.

"Do you know what I'm saying?" she asked.

They stopped walking. As Warren Wright turned to face her, he looked as if he might cry.

"Oh, Dad. I'm sorry. But I must." They hugged gently, released each other, and continued strolling. "Your little girl is a woman now, and she has found her soulmate. Just pretend I'm getting married to a Frenchman. It's like I'll be living in Paris, and you'll be here in Mystic Heights."

"I know," he said. "I think I might want to live in Paris too. It's the city of love. Or so it was."

"I love you, Dad," she whispered. She had broken the news but would not reveal Jack Travers' secret. It would be too much for her father to carry.

"Yes. And I love you, Emma." He looked into her eyes, and they hugged again. Then he released her. Constantly wary, he looked around as if someone might be watching or listening. "The night has a thousand eyes," he muttered, "and the night air is making mine misty. We should head back home."

We're scheduled to be transported to the year 1934. April 9th be exact. This date was picked by Currant. Mission—to stop the political assassination of Franklin Roosevelt to assure that he completes his first term of office, at least. We'll have about two weeks before the home opener to prepare to save the day and two weeks after that date to evaluate the results of our efforts.

Even though it's taken a ton of effort and a lot of luck, we did save the 1932 election for him; we did keep him from being assassinated in 1933, and with a little more good fortune we will return to Washington D.C. and somehow stop him from falling on his face at the home opener. I'd like to see a major league baseball game...never have. The game of professional baseball died in the late 1980s. It was just too slow for the new generation. But I've always liked the concept. It's a thinking man's game. It's like chess with real men for board pieces. And it has to be crazy difficult to hit a ball traveling at 90 miles per hour swinging a cylindrical bat. And then there's the curve ball and the sinker and the knuckleball. Anyway, this coming game will feature Heinie Manush (love that name) in left field for the Senators. Too bad Lefty Grove won't start for Boston. Seeing him pitch would be a once-in-a-lifetime thing.

Emma is <u>very</u> anxious to see Jack Travers again. Apparently, their separation in Miami was a serious tearful event. I've got a feeling she won't be coming back. Tough for Mr. Wright. Hey, who knows, maybe I'll stay too. I may pack my Voicenator. It would be cool to hang out in the old days. Lots of smoke and booze though. I know Currant would. He fits perfectly in the 1930s. And Ethan, he might stay if he wasn't so determined to read about the results of our adventures in The History. We all want to fix the past. Although I'm not convinced that the visible individual players in history are the source of all events. As DuFour suggested, there may be greater forces moving the chess *pieces around the board. But we all want to make the world a better place. It's possible that keeping FDR alive and active may do the trick. He's got big ideas. He's got the people and the Congress behind him. And I don't think he gives a damn about the rich and powerful people who are intent to get rid of him and his "socialistic" ideas. Heck, after he recognized the Soviet Union and established diplomatic relations with the USSR, I think he scared the pants off the rich elite. They're afraid he'll turn communist and nationalize and marginalize the lot of them. No multimillionaire wants to lose all his wealth and status. They will fight to the death. We'll see if we can stop them from toppling FDR. See you at the old ballgame.*

End 03-06-33

-Chapter IV-

Planting the Seed

It was easy to find conspiracies in Washington, thought Jack. Aggressive, scheming people getting together to plan some future event was not a novelty in the nation's capital—just the nature of politics and a give-and-take, scratch my back, and I'll scratch yours attitude. From the standpoint of making money or spreading influence, the typical connivances, a dash of flattery, and a hint of lucre were enough to produce positive results. Washington was a well-oiled, time-tested machine that benefited the politicians, lobbyists, and bureaucrats at the expense of the people. For those in the know, it wasn't advisable to work on the dark side unless it was necessary to modify the system simply to survive. Even those so strongly motivated to cross the boundary and become criminal conspirators would often conceal their true nature by appearing to be conventional lobbyists. Knowing this, Jack Travers was not fooled by the innocuous title of the conference being held at the Mayflower Hotel. He checked the event schedule posted in the lobby—*Saturday, July 1, 1933—The Delaware Room, 2nd floor—Committee for a Sound Dollar and Sound Currency.* Two weeks of serious investigation following his meeting with Mrs. Roosevelt had led him here. Now he had to put his plan into action. He took the elevator, stepped out into a balconied area, and then walked the few steps to the conference room. He passed scores of men on break from their meetings standing in the nearby foyer. They smoked cigars and talked loudly, excitedly barking, bleating, coughing, and spitting like barnyard animals. This political petri dish filled with squirming organisms was a source of amusement for Jack. Involuntarily, he shook his head and smiled. Some things never change, he thought.

He entered the modest conference room overlooking Desales Street. Jack knew conspiracies in their embryonic state were delicate things. Their initial form typically bears little resemblance to the shape they will become. A few men dressed in business suits, a small smoke-filled room, and quiet discussions greeted his senses. But lurking someplace, concealed within the coded conversation and the wary smiles, was the beginning of a large, illegal, traitorous plan to overthrow the government of the United States of America. Strangely, Jack Travers was there to enable it.

"Welcome, friend. Come in," said one of the men.

"Thanks," replied Travers. His eyes scanned the room. Four men, including the man who greeted him, stood talking near the window wall. Travers glanced down. He spotted a table with pamphlets laid out. A placard on the same table proclaimed: *No One Wants a Rubber Dollar! Join the Sound Dollar Committee Today*; a drawing below the writing depicted an artist's image of a smiling President Roosevelt holding a ten-dollar bill in two hands and stretching it as if it were an old inner tube. Jack grabbed one of the pamphlets and scanned it for a minute. The man at the window, mid-thirties with the rather pudgy, pasty look of a hard-drinker and big-eater, smiled at him and then broke away from the other men. He approached Travers and shook his hand.

"Gerry MacGuire. I'm throwing this party." He laughed. "Thanks for stoppin' by. You interested in making this country great again?" When he spoke, he reminded Jack of a ventriloquist's dummy.

Travers smiled. "Who isn't? It's about time, right?"

"It is for me," he said with the confidence of a confidence man. "Didn't catch your name...."

"Quinn. Jack Quinn. Call me Jack."

He leaned in. "OK, Jack. What can I tell you about the 'Committee for a Sound Dollar and Sound Currency?'?"

Jack took a deep breath and stepped back to create distance between himself and the assertive MacGuire. "Well, I happened to be in the building to meet someone regarding a new project of mine, and I saw your announcement outside. I was curious."

"Come on over here and sit down for a moment. Coffee?"

"Sure." Jack moved to the food table and poured a cup. While holding the coffee pot, he looked at the man. "You?"

MacGuire chuckled again. "I'd float away if I had another."

As Jack took a sip of his coffee, he looked closely at his host. The man didn't look dangerous or treasonous.

"Have a seat," said Gerry MacGuire. He led Jack to a couple of wing chairs at the end of the room. They sat. "So, tell me about your project?"

Jack set his coffee cup on a table. He lit a cigarette and then looked back at MacGuire. "I don't know if you'd be interested, but...." He waited.

"Always interested in new ideas, Jack."

"We're birds of a feather. Fact is, you never know until you listen." He took a breath and began. "Anyway, I'm starting a weekly newspaper devoted to veterans. Something like the old *National Tribune*. Remember that?"

MacGuire smiled. "Remember it well, Jack. Started after the Civil War."

"It's still going. Merged with the *Stars and Stripes* a few years back. It still has lots of readers. But I want to give those readers a new insight into the war."

"Did you serve?"

"Yes. I only caught the tail end—II Corps. When we finally got to France, it was all over."

"Lucky boy, Jack. It wasn't fun."

"We're you over there?"

MacGuire smiled. "Over there, over here, over there, and again. I was an ensign on a troop ship. The *Aeolus*. It was an old German tub. The Navy refitted it into a troop carrier. We brought them over and then brought most of them back. Thousands of men. Seems like just yesterday. But what makes you think your magazine can compete with the Legion or the V.F.W.? They've got monthlies already. I'm a Legionnaire. Connecticut. I get 'em every month."

"Well, then you know. There are stories in their magazines and in the *National Tribune*," he said, nodding. "Some of them pretty interesting. But most of their pages are devoted to internal issues. Politics and money-raising. And their audience is limited. I want to put together a monthly for everybody. Filled with stories of heroism and adventure. Quality writers. True stories. I think enough time has passed since the war to emphasize both the glory and reality. Readers want reality now. Look at Hemmingway. Look at Hammett. I don't think it would be too difficult to capture the public's attention with action-filled, true stories of a world at war with American boys fighting to make that world safe for democracy."

MacGuire pursed his lips as if thinking. He had a habit of scratching the top of his head while listening. "Interesting. Got a name?"

"Yes. I call it *American Warrior*".

MacGuire thought about it, then replied, "I like it, Jack. I think it's a great idea. I might know a few people who might be interested. It could be a success. Let's talk about it later with my buddy Doyle. He's gabbin' over there. Another Legionnaire." He nodded at the dark-haired, stiff-lipped older man who was making a point to his listener by tapping his finger into his palm. MacGuire shifted in his chair. "So, what do you think about our new President. As you can guess, our little group is not thrilled with his monetary policy."

Jack pretended to think. "The jury's still out. But he is moving fast. He's got the blood flowing here in Washington."

MacGuire laughed. "Oh. It's flowing in New York too. I'm a bond representative with Grayson M-P Murphy & Company. We're one of the biggest brokerage firms. Our clients are very much concerned about the direction FDR is taking the country. To be honest, many of them think he's walking us straight down the road to Communism. They're concerned about gold confiscation and the potential of unhooking the U.S. dollar from the gold standard. You know, my friend, if we don't have a sound currency, we don't have anything. It will be chaos."

"I'm with you on that," said Jack, "but what will you do? Seems like Roosevelt is in the driver's seat."

MacGuire smiled. He nodded. "He is the President. The American Legion has been kind to FDR. They listened politely to his speeches. Maybe too politely. We're trying to press them for a stand on the gold standard. As I said, I'm a Legionnaire, but I think it's time for new leadership in our organization."

Jack rubbed his chin. "Maybe you should join the Veterans of Foreign Wars. I know nothing about economics, but I do know leadership. You need someone like General Smedley Butler. He stands for the citizen-soldier. He's a big wheel in the V.F.W., and I suspect he doesn't like Roosevelt's policies. He's been trying to get veterans their war Bonus for years. And the way I see it, FDR set Butler and all those old soldiers back a decade with the passage of the Economy Act."

MacGuire appeared to wrestle with this idea. "I know of General Butler. I've thought about him. A bit of a loose cannon, but...."

"That's not what the rank and file say," said Jack. "They love him. I was at the Anacostia encampment when he made his speech. Twenty-five thousand men loved him. They were all gassed and burned out a few days later by Hoover and MacArthur. Back in the trenches in France again. But now, it was in their own backyard. It was all very nasty. From what I read in the newspapers, General Butler is still fighting for these men. He'll never give up."

"Do you ever meet him?" asked MacGuire.

"I met him last year at the rally. The fellow's a real hero. He won two Medals of Honor. The most decorated Marine in history. He's not afraid to speak his mind. He's a soldier's soldier. I listened to his speech, and afterward, I sat with hundreds of others around a bonfire that night, and we swapped war stories. I can't say I got to know him. But I get around to the V.F.W. meetings. And I have a passing relationship. He knows about my *American*

Warrior project. At least I've mentioned it to him. He's a great guy."

MacGuire seemed to go into deep thought. "You might be right."

"How so?" asked Jack.

"General Butler would shake things up. He would be great for the Legion."

"Maybe, but I doubt he would be interested in your organization."

"You mean the Legion or the Committee?"

"I guess neither. Butler's a V.F.W. guy. He's a Bonus guy. Seems like the Legion has other ideas about the Bonus. They don't seem too interested. And insofar as sound dollars are concerned...."

MacGuire seemed undeterred. "You may be right. But I'll bet he is no fan of Roosevelt. How about a repeal of the Economy Act? There's a concept that might grab Butler's attention. You know veterans are committing suicide daily because they lost their pensions. Three hundred thousand vets lost their disability allowances. Some vets are blaming big business for these cuts. But you and I know who did the deed last March. And now FDR's spending all our money on those C.C.C. camps. He's turned his back on the vets."

Jack nodded and downed the last of his coffee. "You're right, Gerry."

"I know I'm right. We've got to straighten this out."

MacGuire stood. Jack set down his coffee cup, snuffed out his cigarette, and got up. MacGuire called his friend, who was introduced as Bill Doyle. After some small talk about the old days, the bond salesman quickly got to the point. "Bill, Jack here is looking for some help to start a magazine full of stories about the war. True stories. Real stories. Something he calls the *American Warrior*. I think it's a good idea. Maybe we can introduce him to a few of our friends. What do you think?"

Jack detected that Doyle's eyes rolled slightly. But he quickly jumped into the conversation. "Sure." He nodded. "Always looking to promote the vets. We need all the help we can get."

"Great, really great," said MacGuire. "Now, get this. Jack here is a friend of General Butler. 'Old Gimlet Eye.' There's a guy we could use. That right, Jack?"

Jack cleared his throat. "Well, I wouldn't say we are bosom buddies, but as I said, we have met."

"Here's the deal, Jack," said MacGuire. "We could really use a man like him to work with our committee. General Butler's been going after that Bonus money for his troops forever. With little to show for it. I mean, the government bounced the Bonus bill out of Congress. After the Bonus March, they chased his vet buddies out of Washington. But I know he still wants it. And I know he'd want his troops paid in real money. The coin of the realm. Not some rubber money that FDR is manufacturing. He'd understand the need to have U.S. money backed by gold. I'm sure of that."

Doyle jumped in quietly. "Jack. Do you think you could make the connection? Our people would be most appreciative."

Jack smiled. "You bet. I could call him right now. If you want."

"Now you're talking. You hear that, Doyle? He can call him right now."

"We could give him a try. I've got his number. He lives in the Philadelphia area. But what are you looking to do?"

"We just want to meet with him," said MacGuire, who was obviously excited by the possibility.

"When?"

"No time like the present. Tell him we're a couple of veterans...and one of us was wounded." He tapped on his head lightly with one knuckle. "Tell him about the silver plate in my head. That will soften him up. Say we want to help him get the Bonus for the vets. That we have an organization behind us. You get it. Just lay it on." He turned to his buddy Doyle. "We could get there this afternoon, right Bill?"

Doyle checked his gold pocket watch. "Absolutely. Not a problem."

Jack shrugged his shoulders. "Get me to a phone. I'll give it the old college try."

"You're a pip, Jack. Thanks. We won't forget you."

MacGuire picked up the phone. Jack handed him a little leather-bound book open to the General's number, and the man passed the request to the hotel operator, asking her to bill the charges to his room. As it rang, he handed the receiver to Jack.

"Hello. General Butler?" And the raspy voice of the old General boomed out. Jack worked the phone like a professional. MacGuire and Doyle smiled in appreciation. Jack recreated a verbal collage of false and genuine memories in vivid detail—the hot afternoon in Anacostia, the bonfire that night, and the several subsequent speeches supposedly he had heard. Smedley Butler was quickly engaged and open. As MacGuire suggested, he laid it on, and the old warrior agreed to meet them later that afternoon.

"Well. That's that! I wish you luck." Jack knew they were hooked as he walked out of the conference room. He thought that he'd better get to know General Smedley Butler. The seed was planted, but he wondered if it would take root.

-Chapter V-

The Pot Boils Over

Jack Travers made his first trip to Milwaukee in the last week of August, 1933. He had secured some fairly realistic press credentials which depicted him as a reporter for his fictitious magazine, the *American Warrior*. Amazingly, he had to admit to himself that the idea had legs. Wherever he went, he told the story of the new magazine. People seemed to like the idea, and they accepted the story and his credentials as fact. On the train coming up from Chicago, he daydreamed that someday he might even turn the cover-story into reality. The title, 'Jack Travers, Publisher' appealed to him. In the meantime, the non-existent magazine served him well. Travers sat in the audience three rows back from the front with a crowd of over four thousand veterans behind him. They gathered together, at this the 34th Veterans of Foreign Wars Encampment, to hear some big-name speakers including General Smedley Butler. Travers hoped to meet that man later.

It was now a month after the two 'sound money' men, MacGuire and Doyle, met with Butler. He wondered about the outcome of that rendezvous, but he didn't want to embroil himself with those two anymore. In time, although they might remember the *American Warrior* magazine, he believed they would forget him and his name. Travers knew these two men had connections to very rich, anti-Roosevelt forces including MacGuire's bond-broker boss Grayson M-P Murphy, a former Army officer who was connected by directorships to many of the largest companies, and who had an excellent relationship with the Morgan banking group. He also knew that Robert Sterling Clark, an heir to the Singer sewing machine fortune, another former soldier and officer in China who had served under Smedley Butler, was a founding financial supporter of the Sound Dollar Committee. Travers suspected the "Committee for a Sound Dollar and a Sound Currency" was a front for a larger group of players with a larger cause.

The identity of these players was no great secret. The anti-Roosevelt forces surfaced at the 1932 Chicago Democratic National Convention when they attempted to broker the convention by delaying and disrupting the nomination. The contender Al Smith, who had run for president in 1928, had enough convention votes to confound the Roosevelt forces. Chicago Mayor Aton Cermak had packed the Chicago Stadium with Smith loyalists. The banking interests, the industrial powerhouses, and the hard-money advocates knew that the popular Franklin Roosevelt would win the nomination, but they wanted to control the event and make him beholden to their interests. Roosevelt had solid support at the convention, but he needed to win a two-thirds majority. Even the rising maverick from Louisiana, Huey Long, supported him at a crucial time in the voting. Travers had heard that Joe Kennedy, helped to swing some of the John Nance Gardner votes to FDR, by convincing the newspaper magnate, William Randolph Hearst, that his influence could make Roosevelt the winner and make Hearst a kingmaker. With the Texan Gardner jockeyed into the V.P. slot, Roosevelt finally won the nomination on the third ballot. Jack Travers had no idea if any deal had been cut with the opposition, but he believed that deal or no-deal, the anti-Roosevelt forces, were now unhappy with short track record of President Roosevelt. They wanted more control or even total control of the Executive office.

Travers suffered through the early-going series of boring V.F.W. administrative proposals. But now the hall was buzzing with excitement. The headliners were about to make their appearances. Members of the House, Gerald J. Boileau and Everett M. Dirksen and Senators Thomas, Robinson, and the one-and-only Huey P. Long were scheduled. But the next speaker was the crowd favorite, the man who came to Washington in 1932 and addressed the Bonus Marchers on that hot July day in the swamplands of Anacostia. When everyone else had abandoned them, he had backed their cause for the release of their World War Bonus money. That afternoon in 1932 Jack, Emma, Ethan, and Zak had listened to his rousing speech. Afterward, General Butler shared company, told war stories and bivouacked with the vets overnight. Now the humble, but great general took to the stage amidst thunderous applause. The Bonus Army would never forget their leader, thought Jack. The man, some called 'The Fighting Quaker,' was not a tall man, nor big, but he was a brave man who spoke the truth. The bushy-browed, hawk-nosed, warrior waited patiently. It took several minutes for the clamor to die down, and then he spoke in a clear, knife-like voice.

"War is a racket," he loudly proclaimed. "It has always been a racket." He paused, stared them down, and waited. The crowd responded noisily affirming his charge. He waited for dead silence, then continued. "It is possibly the oldest, easily the most profitable, surely the most vicious. It is the only one international in scope. It is the only one in which the profits are reckoned in dollars and the losses in lives. A racket is best described, I believe, as something that is not what it seems to the majority of the people. Only a small inside group knows what it is about. It is conducted for the benefit of the very few, at the expense of the very many. Out of war, a few people make huge fortunes."

"In the World War, a mere handful garnered the profits of the conflict. At least 21,000 new millionaires and billionaires were made in the United States during the World War. That many admitted their huge blood gains in their income tax returns. How many other war millionaires falsified their tax returns no one knows. How many of these war millionaires shouldered a rifle? How many of them dug a trench? How many of them knew what it meant to go hungry in a rat-infested dug-out? How many of them spent sleepless, frightened nights, ducking shells and shrapnel and machine gun bullets? How many of them parried a bayonet thrust of an enemy? How many of them were wounded or killed in battle?" He paused. "Not many. Not like you men. But they weren't there. Were they?'

"That's right, general!" a single shout came from the back of the room.

Butler smiled and moved on. "The normal profits of a business concern in the United States are six, eight, ten, and sometimes twelve percent. But war-time profits—ah! That is another matter—twenty, sixty, one hundred, three hundred, and even eighteen hundred per cent—the sky is the limit. All that traffic will bear. Uncle Sam has the money. Let's get it."

"It has been estimated by statisticians and economists and researchers that the war cost your Uncle Sam fifty-two billion dollars. Of this sum, thirty-nine billion was expended in the actual war itself. This expenditure yielded sixteen billion dollars in profits. That is how the twenty-one thousand billionaires and millionaires got that way. This sixteen-billion-dollar profit is not to be sneezed at. It is quite a tidy sum. And it went to a very few."

"But the soldier pays the biggest part of the bill. If you don't believe this, visit the American cemeteries on the battlefields abroad. Or visit any of the veteran's hospitals in the United States. On a tour of the country, I have visited eighteen government hospitals for veterans. In them are a total of about fifty thousand destroyed men— men who were the pick of the nation eighteen years ago. The very able chief surgeon at the government hospital here in Milwaukee, where there are 3,800 of the living dead, told me that mortality among veterans is three times as great as among those who stayed at home. These boys paid the bill and more, didn't they?"

While Butler's eyes glistened with tears, the audience quietly affirmed his statement.

"Boys with a normal viewpoint were taken out of the

fields and offices and factories and classrooms and put into the ranks. There they were remolded; they were made over; they were made to 'about face'— to regard murder as the order of the day. They were put shoulder to shoulder and, through mass psychology, they were entirely changed. We used them for a couple of years and trained them to think nothing at all of killing or of being killed."

"The only way to smash this racket is to conscript capital and industry and labor before the nation's manhood can be conscripted. One month before the Government can conscript the young men of the nation— it must conscript capital and industry and labor. Let the officers and the directors and the high-powered executives of our armament factories—and our munitions makers and our shipbuilders and our airplane builders and the manufacturers of all the other things that provide profit in war time— as well as the bankers and the speculators, be conscripted—to get thirty dollars a month—the same wage as the lads in the trenches get."

"Let the workers in these plants get the same wages— all the workers, all presidents, all executives, all directors, all managers, all bankers—yes, and all generals and all admirals and all officers and all politicians and all government office holders—everyone in the nation be restricted to a total monthly income—not to exceed that paid to the soldier in the trenches!"

Butler sipped from a glass of water while the soldiers before him applauded.

"Let all these kings and tycoons, and masters of business and all those workers in industry and all our senators and governors and mayors pay half of their monthly thirty dollar wage to their families, and pay war risk insurance, and buy Liberty Bonds."

"Why shouldn't they? They aren't running any risk of being killed or of having their bodies mangled or their minds shattered. They aren't sleeping in muddy trenches. They aren't hungry. The soldiers are!"

"I am not a fool as to believe that war is a thing of the

past. I know the people do not want war, but there is no use in saying we cannot be pushed into another war."

With a folded handkerchief, he wiped the sweat from his brow.

"Looking back, Woodrow Wilson was re-elected president in 1916 on a platform that he had 'kept us out of war' and on the implied promise that he would 'keep us out of the war.' Yet, five months later he asked Congress to declare war on Germany."

"In that five-month interval, the people had not been asked whether they had changed their minds. The four million young men who put on uniforms and marched or sailed away were not asked whether they wanted to go forth to suffer and die."

"Then what caused our government to change its mind so suddenly?"

"I'll tell you! It was one thing. M-O-N-E-Y—money."

"I spent 33 years and four months in active military service, and during that period I spent most of my time as a high-class muscle man for Big Business, for Wall Street and the bankers. In short, I was a racketeer, a gangster for capitalism."

"When you came home from the World War, you marched along Fifth Avenue, great heavy masses of men, all your feet moving together, one objective, one cause, all swaying back and forth as you went along. You were a unit. All the people of America applauded. But on the second day, they disbanded you, and they said, 'To hell with you.' Because you were then individuals, and politically the soldiers never amounted to anything. And I say, to hell with war!"

A tremendous uproar of applause ensued. Butler waited, then he continued.

"Right now, we are all called upon to support the administration. I know the soldiers; no matter what you tell them they are always going to support any president up to a certain point, but you must remember that you have two duties. One is to your own flesh and blood, yourself and your family; and the next is your public duty.

Combined is another duty, equally important, and that is the duty to the people, the buddies who served with you, who have been hurt. Go along, do the right thing. We can't afford to bust up this country. Nobody knows where these schemes are going to lead us nowadays. But they won't work if the soldiers don't make them work. You know that. Because we are the class that wins all the wars. Hell—this is a war!"

"You have a difficult role to play because you can't afford to have public opinion against you. At the same time, we must not desert the fellows among us who deserve help. Let me tell you again. Just get together, learn your lessons, be able to say them in your sleep. Get together, follow your leaders. You have never had a leader in this outfit that sold you out, and I don't believe you ever will. When you go down to Washington, you've got to growl and bite!"

"When you soldiers agree to lay aside your petty jealousies and personal ambitions and fight as you fought in wars, you'll get somewhere. Not until then will you get what you want. You've got to get mad! You've got to hate! You've got to turn on these fellows who call you names such as 'treasury raiders.'"

"The only trouble with you veterans is that you still believe in Santa Claus. It's time you woke up—it's time you realized there's another war on. It's your war this time. Now get in there and fight!"

Abruptly, the general saluted the audience and left the stage amidst loud cheering. As the old soldier walked past, Jack caught his eye, nodded and smiled. Butler smiled back.

Meanwhile, the cheerleaders in the audience cried out. "Three cheers for the New Deal!"

The audience responded: "Raw! Raw! Raw!" This chant continued for at least a minute until the next speaker made his way onto the stage.

Jack decided it was time to pay the general a visit. He was able to catch up with him and his entourage in the lobby outside the convention hall. General Butler was enjoying a smoke break. Surrounded by many admirers and a few men who obviously were, at the very least, screeners, Jack checked in with one of the general's men and showed him his reporter credentials. The man told him he would have an opportunity to talk briefly with the general. Loud banter, generated by the Butler's many admirers, filled the room. Shafts of daylight from high windows above sliced through the clouds of cigarette and cigar smoke and shone on the general's face like divine radiance. One of his handlers guided Jack into position in front of Butler. Jack hunched over slightly to align his eyes with 'old gimlet eye.'

"Hello, General. I'm Jack Quinn." They shook hands. There was a hint of recognition in the man's eyes possibly because Jack had smiled at him just a few minutes earlier. "I listened to your speech last year in Anacostia. It was great. I just wanted to meet you in person."

"My pleasure, Jack."

Jack recognized that this was not a new topic of conversation for Butler. It had probably been used as a conversation starter many times today. "Sir, we spoke on the phone a couple of months ago. I called you about two soldiers who wanted to see you. You may remember. Something about 'Sound Money.' Said they could help get the Bonus. One fellow had a silver plate in his head..."

The general lost his smile. He looked into Jack's eyes as if he could see to the back of his skull. "Are you hooked up with those fellows?"

"No." Jack shook his head. "I just bumped into them at the Mayflower Hotel. They thought I could help them with their cause. I hope they didn't inconvenience you. You know how we all try to help each other."

Butler pondered the words. "We do. I do. But I don't know about them. I get many veterans approaching me. These two arrived at my house in a limo. I don't get many visits from their kind. Can't say I want to. They were Legion boys." He paused. "Are you a Legionnaire?"

"No, sir. I'm thinking of joining the V.F.W."

"There is a difference, you know. That's why the V.F.W.

is growing, and the American Legion is shrinking. You're in the right place, son."

"That's why I'm here. Sorry, they bothered you, General."

Butler scoffed. "Listen, son. I'm retired. I can say and think what I want. I'm a big boy. I'm open to all kinds of ideas that might get my boys the Bonus. Something might pan out there. Don't worry about it." As he offered his handshake again, he trailed off with "...pleasure to meet you." Then he turned away to face another group of vets, one of whom had a box camera ready for a photo op. Mission accomplished, thought Jack. He eased his way out through the crowd which had grown considerably.

Apparently, the convention assembly was on lunch break. He worked his way into the auditorium and sat down in one of the chairs in the rear. He left an empty chair between him and two men talking to each other. For the moment, he just wanted to gather his thoughts and rest. The auditorium was hot and stuffy, but as the crowd cleared, the remaining background noise became a comforting unfocused buzz. His mind drifted until a voice broke the spell.

"Hey, Mac. You gotta' light?"

Jack looked to his left at the closest of the two men. Like Jack, they were not wearing V.F.W. uniforms nor caps. And they did not display any patches or medals. They both wore dark suits, red ties and matching silver-colored shirts. "Sure." He pulled out a pack of matches he had picked up in his hotel and handed it to the skinny, rough-looking, late-thirties man. "Keep 'em."

"Thanks. You a member?" he asked.

"No. I'm in the Legion. How 'bout you?" Jack adapted his speech pattern to that of his neighbors.

"We're just checkin' things out."

The other man looked like an older brother for the first. He eyed up Jack with somewhat of a scowl.

"Do you think these guys will back a real patriot?"

"They love General Butler," said Jack as he fired up one of his Luckies. "You know we shouldn't be doing this.

Smoking in here's not allowed."

They laughed. "Everything's not allowed. That's the problem."

"There are a lot of problems out there," said Jack. "What's yours?"

The man thought. He stared at Jack, then answered. "Like everyone. No jobs. No money. The country's got no direction."

"No argument here." He paused. "Like your shirts."

"You noticed. We've been flyin' low. But now we're comin' out. 'Silver Shirts.' Just a little reconnaissance mission today. We're up from Oklahoma."

Jack smiled. The name 'Silver Shirts' rang a bell. "I think I heard of you fellows. No fuzzy edges about your organization."

"Hell no," said the younger man. "You got a problem with us?"

"Nope."

"See this," said the man, then he opened his suit jacket and exposed an embroidered red-letter "L" resting on the right side of his chest. "Loyalty to the United States, my friend. This will be our official uniform. Lyle and I are part of the advance group" he said blowing a cloud of smoke from his cigarette straight up past his nose for effect. "Just like you. We're here to watch and listen."

"Pick up anything new?" asked Jack.

"Nope. The same old stuff. But I'd say that General Butler has a mouth on him. Ya' know not too long ago he called out Benito Mussolini and almost got canned for it. We're not big fans of him."

Jack remembered that General Butler had publicly denounced Italy's dictator as a heartless, reckless man. In response, Butler was sanctioned by President Hoover and the military. But the court martial proceedings were dropped when the news came out that the Italian dictator had indeed driven his car recklessly at high speed, struck a young girl, and left her for dead. Travers knew the truth, but he played along. "You think General Butler's not loyal?"

The man smiled. "He's got the medals, but he's lost in his cause. He doesn't see the big picture. If he could only see how important he could be."

"How's that?'

The man took a deep drag on his cigarette and talked out the smoke. "This country is falling off a cliff. You got that Jew, 'Rosenfeld' in the White House. He's cozied up with the Soviet Commies. And he means to grab this country for them. Then we got guys like Huey Long. He's comin' up to speak later. You'll see. Seems to me, the only difference between him and FDR is his 'good old boy' drawl. He wants to run the show and give away the store. Just like 'Rosenfeld.'"

"What about your guys?"

"My friend, we've got a leader. William Dudley Pelly. You remember that name. He's a great man. He's not like the two-faced Commies running this country. He's gonna' lead our people just like Chancellor Hitler or Prime Minister Mussolini—'El-Doo-chee.'" He smiled. "The leader. If General Butler was smart, he'd get behind our guy. These vets would get that Bonus money quick."

"You think your man has a chance of breakin' into the big time?" asked Jack.

They both laughed. "We're gettin' there, my friend. We'll be across the nation twenty or thirty thousand strong by next year. You'll see. In '36 we'll be a force to reckon with."

Jack dropped his cigarette and snuffed it out with the sole of his shoe. "Gotta' go, guys. Have fun. I think I've had enough."

"Hey, you're gonna' miss the 'Huey Long Show.'"

"A little bit of Huey goes a long way..."

"Amen, brother. Amen."

Jack drifted away. Soon he was out in front of the building enjoying the fresh air, the relative quiet, and the sunshine. In time, he returned to the convention hall.

Later that afternoon, speaker after speaker including the senators and congressmen, derided Roosevelt's

Economy Act. Jack knew this was going to be an unpopular position among the gathered faithful. Speakers labeled the act as the "most cruel, brutal, and utterly indefensible act ever passed by a cowardly Congress." The mood against FDR was building to a crescendo. Again, the hall was filled and bubbled with anticipation. Jack took notice of a disturbance to his right. Huey Long's protection detail was leading the way to the podium. The audience reacted as if a movie star had arrived. Jack got a good look at Senator Long. He was aware that the previous night Long was at a charity event in New York. He also knew that the charismatic senator from Louisiana had been punched in the face after insulting someone at the affair. Even from a distance, it was obvious that the area above his eye had been doctored up and powdered. Long claimed afterward that he was beaten by a gang of men in a washroom. And smelling blood, the local newshounds went after him this morning. No doubt that is why he appeared to be in a foul mood when he commenced his speech.

The pie-faced, fast-talking, political preacher began his monolog. "We've had an exodus of polecats in Louisiana," he shouted throwing a fist in the air, "but when I picked up your Milwaukee newspapers, I knew where all the polecats had gone. In Louisiana, we don't stand for polecats, thieves, rascals and other varmints, like skunks in the woods." He glared at the newsmen below. "Fellows, do I have to put up with this?"

"Get these boys out of here!" he commanded as he pointed to the tangle of news photographers popping flashbulbs in his face. The sergeants-in-arms descended on the newsmen and quickly escorted them away from the stage area. "That's more like it," said Long. He pounded his fist into his other hand. "Say good-bye to the polecats, boys." The senator smiled as he watched the photographers leave.

The crowd cheered wildly. Then the senator glared at the newspaper reporters sitting a table just to the left of the stage, not far from where Jack Travers sat. "Anyone who believes the bull pucky that you fellows write should be bored with a hollow horn."

That got the crowd activated. Hundreds of men stood on their chairs, and dozens of other surged down the aisles. Huey Long waved his hands and shouted, but the noise of the raging crowd was so loud that Travers could not understand his rants. Finally, order was restored.

Long, who had removed his suit jacket, presumably to allow for a greater freedom of expression, began anew. This time he railed against FDR. "Let's talk about Morgan, Wall Street, the Rockefellers and the Baruchs. These guys are the leaders of the gang that runs President Roosevelt. You know I voted for that man. But now I'm not so sure. We don't need a leader who is on such intimate terms with Bernard Baruch. I'll tell you the problem."

"Your government is like a restaurant with only one dish. They've got a set of Republican waiters on one side and a set of Democratic waiters on the other side. But no matter which set of waiters brings you the dish, the legislative grub is all prepared in the same Wall Street kitchen."

"You're right, Huey!" shouted the man standing next to Jack Travers.

"You fellows know you've been had when you're in a poker game and ninety-five percent of the money on the table goes to the big winner. So...do you want a 'new deal'? Good luck, my friends. What are you going to deal with? It isn't going to do any good to break open a new deck of cards and deal another hand. *The man* has gone home with all your money." He opened his arms in a gesture of exasperation and raised his eyes to the heavens.

The audience erupted into laughter and applauded. When the rousing approval died down, he continued. "We need a new program to raise taxes on the rich and redistribute the wealth to the rest of the players. We don't need a 'new deal.' We need to call this crooked game and demand our money be returned. You veterans need to be paid your Bonus! That will get you back in the game!"

The audience cheered loudly and called out his name repeatedly. They stood on chairs and stamped on the floor. Huey Long had captured the heart of the convention. President Roosevelt was lucky he had declined the invitation to speak to this group, thought Travers. They would have skinned him alive like one of Huey Long's polecats.

-Chapter VI-

No Time Like the Present

Even though the cherry blossoms would not reach their peak for another six days, most of the trees surrounding the Tidal Basin were heavy with the smell and colors of spring. Emma and Jack walked along the winding path beneath a speckled pale pink and green canopy. She wore a white cardigan sweater over a crisp cotton yellow dress, her dark brown hair was down, her movement was bouncy, and her attitude was one of enchantment. She leaned back and let the bright sun warm her face while humming a song from one of her favorite early-thirties movies.

"What's that?" asked Jack.

She smiled and began to sing quietly in her lovely voice. "Can it be the trees that fill the breeze with rare and magic perfume? Oh, no, it isn't the trees; it's love in bloom. Can it be the spring that seems to bring the stars right into this room? Oh, no, it isn't the spring. It's love in bloom."

"Very pretty," he said. "Just like you." They stopped briefly, and he leaned in and kissed her lightly.

"You're just like Der Bingle. He sang that to Kitty Carlisle in *She Loves Me Not*. I don't think that movie's been released yet. But you'll see, 'Love in Bloom' will be a big hit."

"Der Bingle? Is that Bing Crosby?"

"That's right. You're catching on. That tune will become Jack Benny's signature song," she said.

Jack shook his head. After giving his mustache a gentle one-two with his thumb and forefinger like a lawyer preparing to make his closing argument, he looked into her eyes and smiled. "Emma, you've got a disease called 'movieitus.'"

"Nope. I'm just in love, my love." She giggled, and he

gave her a hug.

They continued to saunter along the path, looking like a romantic couple out of a movie.

Last night she had surprised him, as much as Jack could be surprised. He returned to his Capitol Hill apartment and found her cooking dinner. When they had parted more than a year ago, Jack, optimistically, had given her a key to his place. At that time, there was no assurance that they would ever see each other again, but neither had doubted that would happen. They were together again, and Emma's dinner was postponed. The separation had made them hungry for more than food. Last night was a wonderful evening. The conversation was limited to sweet talk and happiness. She did complain about his cigarette smoke, and he gently mentioned her not-so-ladylike aggressiveness. But, they laughed at the ridiculous pettiness of their comments, considering that she had traveled hundreds of miles and a hundred years back to be with him and that he had waited alone for more than a year, trusting her to return. From the moment she opened the door to his apartment, the moment she smelled his smell and saw her photograph resting prominently on his nightstand, Emma knew her decision to return to the man she loved was correct. They didn't talk about her family, the Roosevelts, or the state of the world in America in 1934. That could wait. Last night was all about renewing their love. But, now they would have to get to work as a team. Today, they would plan not only their future but also the future of America.

They sat down on a bench facing the Tidal Basin waters. Earlier, they made a pilgrimage to the nearby Lincoln Monument, where they, in the summer of 1932, had first held each other. Now, his arm around her, she was relaxed and at home with this world. As always, this time of year and the cherry blossoms attracted many visitors. They watched the unknowing people wander past. Emma wondered if they had any concept of their world and how wonderful and comfortable it was to be alive at this time. Even with the economic pain, and the daily struggle, life was worth living. These people had a future. She looked back at Jack. "So much has happened. So much..."

"...time has passed?" He said, finishing her sentence. They laughed.

"Stop it. It's time to get serious," she said. "Let's talk about you."

"First you," he said. "Have you broken the news to your family and friends?"

"I haven't told anyone," she answered quietly.

"So, they don't know that I know? You haven't found time to tell them that your fiancée is not a man of this world? You haven't mentioned in passing that in addition to all my other good points, I'm a time-cop from the future?"

She pulled away. "Look, I thought of bringing it out many times. But I never could get started. Anyway, once we were back home, I didn't think it mattered."

He laughed. "Well, there's some optimism. I'm sure your Uncle Arthur would be most interested to know that I was a fellow time traveler. He might just have a few reservations about dealing with me." Jack sat with his hands folded in front of him and turned to look at her. "I never mentioned it, but I know about your team's last encounter with some of our guys."

She looked at him quizzically.

"Dallas. 1963...remember?"

Emma recoiled, yet not knowing why. When Jack had revealed that he too was a time traveler, and even more shocking that he was a time-cop, they had no time to discuss details. She had to return, and neither of them was in the mood to open this can of worms. So, it was left unaddressed. And that last night in Miami in 1933, they both agreed that there were more important things to do. But now, it was the time. The cold reality of Jack's job as a time-cop jumped into Emma's head like a piercing scream.

Thoughts of November 22, 1963, overwhelmed her. "You weren't there? Were you?" she asked.

"No, but I was very close to a co-worker named Joell. You might say he was a mentor of mine. One night over a few drinks, he told me about that day. It was one of the most significant jumps of his long career. He was there to ensure there was no interference with the upcoming assassination of President John Kennedy. The big event was strictly a local time affair, but just in case, he was there to watch for rogue time travelers. He knew that something had gone wrong with the Chicago attempt to kill JFK, and his job was to make sure nothing like that happened in Dallas. He located the unauthorized time travelers the morning of the murder. An older guy and three teens. Two boys and a girl. According to him, they got away. Some other time-cops who made the trip didn't make it back. These guys were an assassination team from the future. They were the backup plan if the local conspiracy failed. Joell suspected these cops tracked down the rogues. But, their plane crashed. You don't know anything about that, right?"

She thought, retreated into sadness, and stared at the water. "I know. I saw them go down. It was a terrible day for everyone."

"My buddy Joell gave you a break. Didn't he?"

"I guess so," she said with resignation, "I never met him. Dr. Currant spoke with him."

"Well, that's another story for another day. The good thing is that he didn't file a report on your group. Apparently, he and Dr. Currant bonded. Joell cut you some slack. But you were lucky they sent me to Washington in 1932 as a stabilization scout. If someone else had shown up, you would have been grabbed unless he fell in love with you as I did. And Mr. Roosevelt most likely would not have been elected. Even if he had won, he would have been eliminated before the inauguration. We all know he didn't become President of the United States until certain time-traveling busybodies appeared."

Emma squinted her eyes and made a face. "So, you never ratted on us?"

"No, 'Rocco.' I didn't squeal," he said, imitating the

voice of a movie gangster.

"Don't make fun," she pleaded.

He grabbed her hand. "I created phony reports. I'm good at that. It's possible the home office suspects I've somehow interfered with *The History* or made a mistake, but they have no proof. They've got a lot on their plate. Things may be breaking down back there. I can sense it. The system is falling apart. I suspect they can't hold it together anymore. But everything changed once you and your comrades waltzed into Anacostia that fated July day in 1932. I have to tell you I've thought about this situation plenty since you left. I wanted you back, but I didn't want to be a part of any more interference with past events."

"Why not? We only want to make the future a better place," she said.

"You assume that will happen. No one can predict an altered future. After we first met, I decided I wouldn't help you and your friends. But once you got sick, I knew I had to become involved. Now, I'm your partner. You're more important to me than anything else. So, I'll listen to your stories of the future, and I'll attempt to be a good husband...fiancé...or whoever."

Emma pulled away again, this time feigning indignity. "Why Jack Travers, I certainly hope you would attempt."

"Emma, I didn't mean it that way. But you're a troublemaker. We don't need to turn over any more tables."

She smiled. "I'm inquisitive, persistent, and right. One more table, my love. One more."

"Have you told your father that you're staying here? I mean, staying in this time? Not going to return?"

"I did."

"And the others?"

"No," she winced. "It's a big deal." Her mind drifted.

Jack nodded. "Yeah. Let's walk."

They walked along the Tidal Pool path. A light breeze tickled the waters, creating an impressionistic scene of fluffy cherry trees under a clear blue sky punctuated by the Capitol building dome and the Washington

Monument. She talked as they walked. "Now, for the big news. Get ready to write some more phony reports to your boss." They walked toward Jack's parked car, and she related the entire tale about FDR's upcoming tragic fall at the ballpark and the resultant political change.

"Humph," he grunted. "This is the nature of time travel manipulation. Not good. And I suppose you want to fix things so that Mr. Roosevelt remains in office and effective?"

"Is it wrong?" she asked.

"It's not a question of right or wrong. Only time will tell. The system has a way of self-correcting. It might be best for the world to leave well enough alone. I understand why you find our world of the future less desirable than this world of 1934. I understand completely. But how do you know that the future will change positively for everyone in this world? Because you, your brother, and your friends have made assumptions? You won't be going back to the future. Neither will I. We'll create a new life here. But your brother, Zak, and Dr. Currant will return, and they, along with your father, will face the aftereffects of what you do here."

They stopped in front of Jack's car. She faced him and grasped his upper arms. "Don't you agree the train has gone off the tracks in our time?" she asked.

He looked at her and rolled his eyes. "I agree with nothing and everything." He walked to the driver's side and opened the door of his new, sand-colored 1934 Chrysler Airflow.

She slid across the seat, and he joined her. He sat with his hands on the steering wheel while Emma leaned back and stared out the windshield. They didn't talk. The distant cherry blossoms hung over and curled around the body of water like a pink doily. Two white swans drifted on the pool. For a moment, she forgot about the future. She rolled down the window to let a cool spring breeze in. "Smell that air. See those trees. The water. Isn't it beautiful, Jack?"

He looked at her. His eyes revealed a gentle affection.

"You're a dreamer, Emma. And your dreams are my dreams. I don't care about the future. I care about us. I have a feeling that if we succeed with your plan to save FDR, we will never be bothered by anyone from the future. I'll go out on a limb. I've spent a lot of time talking to Mrs. Roosevelt. I'm convinced that, given the opportunity, she and her husband will change the face of our future. That world will be gone forever. But, if your plan fails, whatever it is, we may just find ourselves facing the worst possible 'realignment' procedures that MOM can force upon us. You get that, right?"

Emma thought before answering. "All the more reason to make it happen, Jack."

He started the engine. "Something else..." he muttered.

"What?"

"I think I'm being followed."

"By whom?"

"I don't know. Even this morning, when we left my place, a car followed us. I'm pretty cautious."

"You're making me nervous. Do you think someone is tailing me?"

Jack scratched the back of his head. "No, this has been going on for a couple of weeks. But I'm not taking any chances. If someone tails me, I don't want them to connect you and me with your brother and your friends. I'm going to drop you off downtown. You're going to walk around. Pretend to shop. Make sure you're not being tailed. Then take a taxi to the hotel. I'll call you tonight."

-Chapter VII-

Groping for Greatness

Ethan grudgingly accepted the fact that they had all slept late today. Their excursion from the future to 1934—the time travel, the endless train ride from Mystic Heights, and the enormous anticipation of the challenge ahead depleted their energies and softened their resolve. A solid sleep had filled him with strength. His good friend Zak had just returned from a walk, which he described as a way to suck up the flavor of depression-era Washington, D. C., giving him an opportunity to girl watch. Now, he sat on the sofa, his feet resting on the coffee table, reading the local newspaper's sports section and occasionally mumbling about his desire to see a real baseball game. He seemed happy, lost in the moment, and strangely unconcerned about the serious work ahead.

A.C. Currant had also exhibited a similar lack of urgency. He had ordered room service breakfast and lounged in his pajamas until noon. But now, he was fully dressed, wearing a dark gray business suit complete with a classic royal blue tie gracing the front of a starched white shirt. A pair of polished black oxfords completed the look. Ethan was always amazed that the physicist seemed to enjoy wearing the period costumes of the thirties. Lately, he started spouting out the catchphrase made famous by the bandleader, Ben Bernie, who would always say 'Yowsah, Yowsah, Yowsah' in his act. Currant also smoked cigarettes like a native. On this trip, he was into Chesterfields. Every time he lit one, he blew out the smoke for effect. Then he would say in a sonorous voice like a radio announcer, "always buy Chesterfield...they satisfy". This little *bon mot* amused him greatly.

But smoking was a habit Ethan could barely tolerate in the open air and one that brought tears to his eyes in the confines of the hotel room. Nevertheless, as part of his

1930s costume, Ethan kept a pack of Camels in his shirt pocket for decoration. He wouldn't smoke, but he would look the part. Currant was into his role. He maintained a near-perfect sartorial consistency and overall temporal authenticity. Before their 1932 trip, Ethan, Zak, and Emma had studied dozens of old black and white movies from the early thirties. They honed their accents, demeanor, and verbal expressions until they became one with the time. But none of them could deal with the practice of cigarette, pipe, or cigar smoking. They disliked the smell, the smoke, and its lung-crippling nature. They could handle the spittoons, the incessant traffic noise, and the air pollution, but social smoking would never become part of their act.

Ethan was full of anxious energy as he sat looking out the window of the Mayflower Hotel suite. His five-story high perch provided an enticing view up tree-lined Connecticut Avenue towards Dupont Circle. The street below was full of noisy, antique automobile traffic. Streetcar bells echoed from building to building. Newsboys hawked their papers, shouting out their headlines, and pigeons that hung out on the window sills of the hotel building cooed incessantly. As Ethan sipped from a glass of iced cola, lost in thought, he ignored the din outside and contemplated the task ahead. It appeared formidable. Their intelligence resources seemed limited, their contacts few, and their opportunity to successfully enter into and change the flow of historical events seemed a hazy fantasy. He wondered where they should start? He failed to gain insight from his thinking, and his friends' lack of activity frustrated him. As he rechecked his watch, his eyes wandered across the street and sidewalks below, then he looked back at Zak. "Where the heck is she?" he asked.

"Cut her some slack. They haven't seen each other for over a year. And you know...." Zak Newman smiled as he signed. His waving fingers talked silently and ended interlocked and rhythmically moving suggestively.

Ethan frowned. He struggled with Zak's not-so-subtle

hint of the intimate aspects of his sister's love affair with Jack Travers. He was working on it, but he remained somewhat embarrassed whenever there was a suggestion of the couple's romantic reality. "I get that. The lovebirds are engaged. I imagine they're making up for lost time. But we have the President to save."

"She must be having a good time. She's not going to be staying here, right?"

"No. She'll be at Jack's place. But she said she would be back here by early afternoon."

"Gentlemen, let's move on," said Dr. Currant. "We're big boys. We can make decisions without Emma. Let's sit and talk." They took positions around the small table in front of the window. "That's better. We have less than two weeks to figure this out and fix it." Currant lowered his head, pushed his salt and pepper hair back with both hands, looked up, and then spoke. "We've agreed that Mr. Roosevelt's fall at the ballpark was not just an accident."

Ethan regrouped mentally. "Had to be intentional," he said. "We know he had fallen in public before, but thanks to the quick reactions of his handlers, those incidents always looked like he just stumbled and then recovered. We also know that the true nature of his physical disability was unknown to the American people. Reporters and cameramen had an unwritten code not to release photos of him in his wheelchair, or images of him wearing his steel braces, or the biggest taboo...photos of him being carried from place to place."

"And I don't believe the people wanted to know," said Currant. "The public believed he was a strong, vigorous leader. Most people's only close encounter with President Roosevelt was via the radio. And he was a master communicator. It was a grand illusion, boys. A blend of mass denial, orchestrated deception, and skillful presentation by FDR. He looked physically strong and capable, and everyone agreed."

"Except after that newsreel..." signed Zak.

"No denying that. We've all seen it. The President goes down like a felled tree. Then he's out of the picture until his handlers pull him up."

"Why was that newsreel ever shown to the public?" asked Ethan.

Currant stared out the window as if looking for the answer, then he turned to face Ethan. "I think that was the second part of the conspiracy. From what we know, FDR loved publicity as long as it was carefully managed. He promoted all opportunities to show that he was a leader in control. Photo ops. That's why there are so many images of him driving a car, playing water polo, and sitting at his White House desk looking like a commander-in-chief. The news cameramen had to submit all their photos to FDR's handlers as part of an official pool of photos. It was easy for FDR's staff to cull out any photo hinting at weakness."

"Right. The baseball game was another photo op. There were photographers and at least a few newsreel cameras," Ethan said. "But thankfully, for FDR, no images appeared. His people must have clamped down on the newspapers. But that one newsreel film somehow ended up in the movie theaters. That was more than enough. Once the newsreel was shown on the west coast, it struck like lightning with audiences. Soon it was seen across the nation and then all over the world."

"A.C. is right. This was part of the plot to take down FDR," signed Zak.

"So, it seems," said Currant. "The plotters had to have been certain that the newsreel would be seen. Otherwise, all their work to make FDR take a dive would accomplish nothing. They must have pulled a fast one on Roosevelt's screeners. According to our good friend DuFour, the film had to be transported out of Washington by airplane. Just two days after FDR took his dive, it appeared in a few theaters in Los Angeles. Roosevelt's team had no response except to claim foul play and declare the newsreel company was profiteering in bad taste. The political goodwill and the grand illusion that FDR had created over the previous decade were shattered by this revelation."

"Once that ball got rolling, there was no stopping it, I

guess," said Ethan. "But the ball won't roll if FDR's braces don't fail when he throws out the game ball on opening day. That's our job, guys."

Zak and Currant nodded.

Just then, there was a knock at the door. Zak answered it, and Emma came breezing into the room.

"Glad you could join us," said A.C. Currant. "We were just discussing the fate of the world."

Emma sat at the end of the bed. "Oh, A.C., you are so dramatic."

"How's Jack?" signed Zak.

"Wonderful. Just wonderful." She leaned back on the bed and then bounced up. "Jealous?"

Zak didn't answer. He simply made a face.

"Well, I'm glad you're back. We can get down to some serious planning now," said Ethan. He got up from his chair and moved to the sofa. "Sit next to me, Emma. Give us the Jack report."

She sat beside him while the other two positioned their chairs in front. Emma recounted her morning and early afternoon activities with Jack. When she mentioned Jack's new car, Zak asked for all the details; he had never heard of the Chrysler Airflow and wanted to see it. Emma's news report didn't sound too exciting to Ethan, but he wasn't romantically engaged. Ethan's eyes focused on the silver engagement band on her finger as she talked, wondering when his sister's involvement with Jack Travers would end. He didn't have to wait long to get his answer. She stopped talking for a moment and seemed to be gathering her thoughts. Haltingly, she spoke. "I don't know how to deliver the news to all of you."

"What news?" asked Ethan.

"Well, I actually have two bits of news." Her voice was that of a mischievous school girl in the principal's office. "I guess I'll start with the easy one." Then she blurted out, "I'm going to stay here and live with Jack."

Mentally, Ethan was trying to catch up. "Stay here when?'

She swallowed. "I'm not leaving 1934. I'm not

returning home to the future."

"That's the easy news?" signed Zak.

"Emma Callan-Wright, does your father know about this?" demanded A.C. Currant.

"He knows. He doesn't like it, but he understands. And I hope you will also."

The concept was becoming clear to Ethan now. His brain moved to a dead stop. Then he attacked. He told her this would be a gigantic mistake. He said that they would never see each other again. He tried to discredit Jack but quickly determined that was not a good approach. He kept up his word battering for several minutes until he had talked himself out. In the end, Emma simply smiled.

"I love you too, brother. But I love Jack very much. And I love these times. I see no future in the future. Other than you guys, Dad, and a few other people, I don't fit. That world is colorless, lifeless, and bleak compared to this time. I want to help create a new world." She paused and smiled. "And I want Jack in that world. I don't expect you to understand. First, you're not a woman. And secondly, you're not in love."

At this point, the conversation slowed to a halt. Zak, Ethan, and Currant just looked at each other speechless.

Zak, who, in fact, was speechless, regained his composure. He quizzed Emma, *"What was the 'hard' news?"*

Emma rolled her eyes. "Umm...maybe it should wait...."

"No. I don't think so, Sis. Let's clear the air," said Ethan with authority. "Are you pregnant?"

She began to laugh, so much so that tears filled her eyes. "Wow! There you go. Making up stories. Of course, I'm not pregnant. But if I were, you would become an uncle. Uncle Ethan. That would bring a smile to the face of any little boy or girl. Anyway, that wouldn't be so terrible."

"What?" he asked in exasperation. "What's next?"

She shook her head. "You guys aren't going to like this."

They waited.

She hesitated, then spoke. "Jack...Jack is a time-cop."

There was another significant pause. Currant was the first one to break the stupor. "Are you making a bad joke?"

Emma cleared her voice, puckered her lips, clenched her teeth, raised her brow, and shook her head gently. "Nope. He's a time-cop."

"This is too much," said Ethan. "What are you talking about?"

"I am saying that Jack Travers has admitted to me that he is a time-cop."

"When did that happen?" asked A.C. Currant.

"I don't know. All the time we've known him, Jack's been a time-cop."

"And you just found out?" asked Zak.

Emma raised her left eyebrow and cocked her head. "Err...not exactly. I found out in Miami. Just before we returned."

"Miami!" exclaimed Ethan. "Are you kidding? And you didn't tell us?" He was almost shouting.

"Sorry. But I had many things on my mind. The fact is Jack is a time-cop. But you might say he's a fallen-away cop. He pretends to do his job, but he is no longer one of them. He's totally on our side."

"How can you be sure?" asked Currant. "What's his mission? Have you told him everything? About the *TimeTravelle*? About us?" Currant was starting to sound frantic.

"I know because Jack has told me. As far as I know, he was sent here in 1932 as a preventive measure. His job was to assure that *The History* was not altered," replied Emma.

Currant stood and then paced around the hotel room. "Give me a second. Jack is on our side. So, you say. For some strange reason, MOM hasn't dragged him back to our time. Is that right?"

Emma thought for a moment. "I really can't say. I don't think he's returned since we first met him at Anacostia.

But I don't know for sure. We can ask him."

"So, once he met you, he fell head over heels and abandoned all reason."

"Something like that..." she said slowly. "We fell in love. I got terribly sick. Jack saved my life..."

"How? You mean when he grabbed you on the night Hoover burned out the marchers?" asked Ethan.

"Yes. He took me to the hospital. And after that, he gave me medicine from the future which cured my T.B."

"And what about us? Did he know what we were up to?" asked Ethan.

Emma smiled. "He's a time-cop...or he was. I'm afraid he was on to the three of us from the beginning back on the flats of the Anacostia. And when you returned in 1933 with our dear 'Uncle Arthur,' he saw an opportunity to help us fix the future. And he did." She raised her hands and shrugged her shoulders in a gesture of release. "He's a time-cop gone bad. MOM thinks he's playing the game straight. Doing his job. He didn't stop the Bonus March from creating martial law. The fact is, if anyone can take responsibility for that, it would be Branko. And he didn't stop FDR from being shot. That honor goes to Dr. Currant. Jack's hands remain relatively clean as far as messing with *The History*."

"The only thing he didn't do was turn the three of us in. Let's face it. We've been lucky. First, that time-cop in Dallas gave us a pass. Jack knew him. He heard the whole story from the man himself. You remember Joell, Dr. Currant."

Currant nodded. "Interesting man..."

"He's dead now," said Emma. "We're fortunate that he and Jack kept us a secret. Otherwise, we'd be dead. And we've been watched over by Jack since we took on this quest to make Franklin Roosevelt President. To the extent we have succeeded, whatever that means, we've been just plain lucky. And we owe Jack.

Currant returned to his seat. He appeared calmer now, almost at peace. He looked at each of the three one at a time, then spoke. His voice was steady and slow. "It all makes sense now. You're right, Emma. We've been lucky. And I've been a fool. Although you three take the cake for your excursion to 1932 when you stole my machine. But I'll take the booby prize for the rest. Dallas in 1963 was a giant reach." He shook his head. "We did save my brother, and I was happy to meet my parents back then. And your father can walk normally because of us. So, some good but...I don't know. This whole quest has been crazy. What I do know is that I promised your father to keep you safe. We can't rely on Jack. He could be exposed as a turncoat at any moment. We have to return. Logically...that's all we can do. We have to go back home."

Having listened to Currant's concession speech, it was Ethan's turn to stand. He shot up from the sofa like a giant jack-in-the-box. "I don't think so, A.C. We didn't come this far to turn back. Emma has brought us good news. We now have an inside man. Jack's a triple agent. He's a time-cop. He's an FDR aide. And he's our co-conspirator. And I trust the guy. Emma's in love with him. And you seem to respect him. And Zak...Zak likes Jack's new car. So, we're covered. Let's move on. We'll save FDR. We'll return home and reap the benefits of our efforts along with the rest of society. And my dear sister Emma will marry and live happily ever after."

A.C. Currant looked up at Ethan and chuckled. "What have you been smoking?"

These few minutes were only the beginning of the conversation. The time travelers talked on for hours that night. Room service fed their bodies, and dogged determination filled their minds. The debate was over. They decided they would push this to the end. As a team, they accepted that Jack Travers could be trusted. They would work with him to stop those on the dark side from co-opting Franklin D. Roosevelt, the thirty-second President of the United States of America. Saving FDR would save the future for everyone. Ethan believed this; it had become his religion.

LOG of Zak Newman
April 10, 1934 (local time): 23:45 (day 2 of time travel)

A.C. Currant and Ethan are down at the hotel bar taste testing post-Prohibition booze. Emma went back to Jack's place. And I spent the last hour reading some newspapers, trying to get a handle on the whole FDR situation. He's a man on a bubble. Last year he won by a landslide. He could do no wrong then. He had a mandate. He got Congress to pass all kinds of laws and create a new type of government. He had the total support of the people, Congress, and the media. But now, things are different.

The New Deal is turning into the raw deal for some. And they're not shy about expressing their disappointment and distrust. The honeymoon is over. The word "commie" is showing up in polite conversation. His NRA program to control prices and wages appears to be unraveling into a socialistic-type bureaucratic nightmare. Those NRA blue eagle signs are everywhere in the windows of storefronts, offices, and factories. But much of this seems to be window dressing. People are grabbing at the straws FDR tosses out. On our train trip down from the north, we saw the hoboes, the breadlines, the hungry, and the disenfranchised. Poverty and pain have not disappeared since the election of Franklin Roosevelt. These are very sad times. On the positive side, it does seem like the workers have a bit more clout, child labor is on its way out, and the workweek is shrinking. But the big guys have taken to government-approved price fixing while the little shopkeepers are battling bureaucratic red tape.

FDR's Civil Works Administration program, designed to provide temporary employment for unskilled workers, ended last week. It costs $200 million a month. Lots of money in these days. It probably saved many people's lives and gave them hope, but the public may not be ready for a welfare system—even if those who get the money have to work for it. Four million people were put to work building roads, schools, parks, and sewers. Then the government ran out of cash. Now they're back on the street. What do you do with all these unemployed people? The economic system is still on life support.

Roosevelt is trying all kinds of tricks. He is a man of action who promotes a broader definition of liberty. He says that the Constitution of the U.S. must be flexible to suit the needs of the people (at least in 1934, they are still concerned about such things). Last year he confiscated all the gold in the country, and he devalued the dollar in an attempt to get prices and wages to rise. For a while, things seemed to be working. Industrial production rose from an index number of 59 to over 100 five months into his term of office. A few months later, it was back in the low 70s.

While millions of pigs are being slaughtered on government orders to keep pork prices up, there have been massive strikes of California farm workers trying to earn a living wage. Giant dust storms are blowing around the middle of the country, blackening the sky, destroying crops, and uprooting people. Hurricanes have crushed coastal areas. The natural disasters are not FDR's fault, but those people affected by all this pain are undoubtedly unhappy.

The tide of public opinion may be turning. Today I saw a joke in the newspaper about a psychiatrist who died and went to heaven. Immediately he was put to work to have a session with God himself. His diagnosis...God suffers from delusions of grandeur. He thinks he's Franklin D. Roosevelt. To the wealthy, the President is a dilatant rich guy who is a traitor to his class. And at the bottom of the ladder are many who are just plain hungry and tired. FDR's economic experiments do not feed their families.

Unemployment remains over 21%. Many of these people are looking to other leaders like Senator Huey Long. To them, Huey seems to be one of them—a common man just trying to make a buck and feed his family. Some, on both sides of the economic fence, may be looking longingly at Germany's Hitler and admiring his apparent 'economic miracle.'

I can see why Roosevelt is on thin ice. He's got a nice smile, and he's very smooth, but facts are facts. This country is on the ropes. Both rich and poor are frustrated, and given the opportunity, they might turn on him.

End 04-10-34

-Chapter VIII-

Hi-Hat

Jack Travers spent the afternoon cleaning his apartment. Located a few blocks southeast of the Capitol building, the smart but small English-basement unit was a great bachelor pad, but if Emma was going to stay, Jack knew they would have to find a larger place. He dismissed this thought from his head. It was too soon to make plans. He and Emma were about to put a wrinkle in time that might turn everything upside down, including their nascent plans for marital bliss. He had a full plate of mostly duplicitous activities. His work for Mrs. Roosevelt had gone well in the past. Last year's Miami resolution pleased her very much. He had somehow managed to keep her husband alive and in office. For this, she rewarded him with a nice bonus which he quickly converted into his new car. His latest assignment did not allow for progress meetings with his boss. She expected him to perform behind the scenes without evidence of her or her husband's involvement. Even in the 1930s, 'plausible deniability was a popular and convenient position. Jack also understood he was operating without a net. If he failed, he would suffer a hard landing; nevertheless, he was reasonably comfortable working with his fiancée and her friends. Emma had blended nicely into the Washington social/political scene, and he had no doubt this would continue.

His thoughts drifted back to life with his lovely Emma. In a month, her brother and her friends would return to the future, disappearing from the present and no longer open to the danger of exposure. Emma could continue her work for Mrs. Roosevelt. And maybe if he worked the system well, he could secure a permanent and more traditional position in the Roosevelt administration. Of course, he would also have to undo his ties to his masters in the future. Theoretically, this was possible. There were rumors of time travelers who had successfully relocated to the past, rogues who had 'disappeared' themselves either by feigning death or simply getting lost. As far as he could tell, based on the transmission and reception of coded messages, he was still on good paper with his controllers. He kept them updated regarding his activities, and they never hinted at any question of his loyalty. But he had been operating in the field for a very long tour. Anytime, they could demand that he come in from the cold. If he were going to defect, it would have to be soon. Then he and Emma might have to relocate from Washington. That might be the only way to escape. But he hoped for another path because this was now his home. He liked it.

He sat at his desk and viewed the garden through the bay window. The last low light of the day bounced off the windows of neighboring buildings enlivening the courtyard. He closed the white wooden window blinds and switched on the Tiffany lamp. Time to go to work, and time for a Lucky. He lit his cigarette and reached into a deep drawer in his desk which housed his communicator device. For the next fifteen minutes, he composed and then transmitted a message to the future, updating them about the bond salesman MacGuire. Months had passed since he had introduced the bulky bond broker to General Butler, but more recent legwork had revealed that MacGuire was on an extensive tour of Europe. Travers suspected he was on a fact-finding mission gathering intelligence about political action groups' potential for the re-mobilization of war veterans. Jack knew that fascism in Europe was enabled by marshaling such forces in Italy and Germany, something Mrs. Roosevelt feared would come to America.

Jack's messages to the home office spun a good tale of intrigue to convince them that his finger was on the pulse of the Roosevelt political team. Some of what he related was contrived; some items were fact. By now, he felt he was writing a serialized novel rather than a continuing police report. He had been spinning a tale for almost two years. Of course, his version, except for the details, would be consistent with the new *'History'* as it developed. His masters were dealing with a history that now included Franklin Roosevelt as President. Jack was their 'boots on the ground' to provide the background for all the current events. He and they knew that, over time, historical events tend to self-correct to achieve some temporal balance. At the moment, the controllers in the future believed that FDR would soon be massaged into political oblivion, allowing more robust, traditional, and reliable approved forces to seize the day. Although they had not provided the details of FDR's demise, Emma had revealed the time and location of the upcoming 'soft *coup*' to Jack.

Jack didn't hint at his foreknowledge of coming events in this evening's communication to the future; he played it straight. He knew everyone working in the past for MOM was supposed to be on a 'need-to-know basis,' and in the minds of his controllers, Jack Travers did not need to know about the upcoming events. Whether they had begun to distrust him or were just cautious, he didn't know, nor did he care. In this case, his supposed ignorance of the future was a preferred state of being. They would not be relying on him to monitor the coming momentous events. The fact that he was not assigned to control the continuity of historical events opened the possibility that another or others had been given this task. Jack, like all time-cops, was accustomed to compartmentalized operations. It was the nature of the beast. But suspecting this, he knew he and Emma would have to remove themselves from the activities leading to and surrounding 'Operation Opening Day': Jack's unofficial name for the conspiracy to politically assassinate Franklin Roosevelt.

After he had secured his communicator inside the desk, he cleaned himself and dressed for the evening. Before leaving the apartment, he left a note for Emma at the base of the Tiffany lamp. He told her he would be back before ten that night. Then he headed out and fired up the Airflow. As he pulled away from the curb, he smiled to himself. The big straight-eight delivered. It was quite a change from his old Buick. This car was futuristic and fast. It was so different from other cars that the public was stunned by its streamlined looks. But Jack didn't mind the attention. He loved this car. As he drove north, he checked his rear-view mirror. The cars behind him zig-zagged and wiggled like wild mice in a maze. Their headlights bounced about in a frenzy. Jack liked the joy these 1934 drivers brought to their rides. One car in the crazy quilt of motion caught his attention. This was his tail. He and that car played cat and mouse for about ten minutes. Then Jack decided it was time to put an end to the game. When he reached K Street, he turned left, drove a few blocks passing Franklin Square, and parked on the street across from the Ambassador Hotel.

In a matter of seconds, the car that was tailing him continued past. Jack pretended to be checking his gauges. Out of the corner of his eye, he could see that the driver, not glancing in his direction, simply drove on. Jack got out, dodged traffic, and crossed the street approaching the hotel entrance. A quick look gave him a view of the tail car making a left turn at the next intersection. He entered the hotel and walked into the bright lights of the Ambassador's lobby. He had been here before, and he was familiar with the layout. It was full of active people and their smells: cigars, sweat, perfume, and chlorine. Jack heard the echoing voices and splashing sounds of guests frolicking in the hotel swimming pool on the floor below and others exiting the elevators, talking loudly, joking, and laughing. A bell rang at the reception desk, and a short young man dressed in a spiffy outfit, including the requisite monkey hat, scurried to claim the luggage of a new arrival. The Ambassador was a hotel for the people. Built near downtown a few years earlier, three bucks a night for a decent room with a bath made it a bargain. Aside from the pool, it offered a brand-new post-Prohibition cocktail lounge on the top floor called the 'Hi-Hat.'

Jack smoked and waited, but not too long. As he anticipated, his tail arrived. The man entered the lobby and quickly searched for his quarry. He was a big, rangy man, late twenties, a few inches over six feet, his light brown hair slicked back. His broad face was evenly tanned and bore squint lines that cut deep into the flesh. He had a casual look about him. His single-breasted, two-button sports coat hung limp and shapeless on his lean body. A patterned tie competed with his checkered jacket and was a tad too loose to be proper. He looked like a man uncomfortable with the times, like someone searching for a sartorial niche. He wore a tan cowboy hat to complete the costume and remembered to remove it upon entering. He held it in front of him with two hands as if he was concealing his private parts. For a man trying to blend in, he stood out like a fan dancer in a convent.

Jack snuffed his cigarette in a nearby urn and smiled at the man. Their eyes finally met, completing the connection, and Jack called him over with a curling forefinger. Almost sheepishly, the big man approached. Jack had no concern that the man might cause trouble. This most public place was inappropriate for a strong-arm approach. If first impressions meant anything, his initial response to the arrival of his new acquaintance was one of curiosity, not concern.   "Well, welcome to the Ambassador. Might I suggest we have a drink? They just opened the cocktail lounge upstairs. It's supposed to be pretty snazzy."

The man appeared puzzled.

"Don't worry; I don't bite. We'll make it Dutch."

He seemed to relax. "I get it." He spoke with a drawl. He extended his hand to shake. "Tom Braedon."

"Jack Travers. But I'm sure you know that."

They took the elevator non-stop to the twelfth floor, saying nothing, but carefully eyeing each other on the way up. Another lobby opened to their view, and Jack walked confidently toward the noise. The Hi-Hat cocktail lounge was open for business. On this evening, like every night since its opening, the public starved for a legal drink and a good time quickly filled the vacuum of thirteen years of government-enforced sobriety. The two men pushed through the glass doors. The club decor was a 'modern' collage of bright stainless steel and yellow and blue accents. The place was jumping with alcohol-induced excitement, filled with smoke, illuminated by smartly concealed fluorescent fixtures, and vibrating with loud music from a live band.

"Seems like a big hit," Jack shouted above the din. Tom Braedon nodded. They checked their hats and then waded through a sea of people. All the seats at the bar were occupied, so the two men staked out a corner. Eventually, an overworked bartender took their order. Not knowing or caring, they let him decide on their drinks. He arrived with two 'Old Smoothies', which apparently was a specialty of the house. The noisy spectacle of people in a frenzied release didn't give them much opportunity to talk.

They both smoked, sipped and surveyed the scene for about ten minutes. Many attractive women cast an eye toward the two handsome and apparently unattached men at the bar. However, Jack and Tom only acknowledged their attention with weak smiles. Meaningful conversation was nearly impossible, but the small talk assured them that this would be a diplomatic meeting. Jack knew who he was dealing with now. After knocking down the drinks, he suggested they might find the lobby outside more conducive to conversation. In a gesture of comradeship, he paid the bar tab.

Outside in the lobby, they found two chairs in a quiet spot and dropped into them. Jack reached into his inside vest pocket, pulled out a small pad of paper and a pencil, and wrote a message in cursive. His handwriting was impeccable. *"If you can't decipher this writing, you are either illiterate or a visitor from another world."* He tore off the sheet, smiled, and handed it to his new drinking buddy. "Would you mind reading this to me?"

Tom Braedon gave the writing a blank look. He stared at it and then gave up. "You're a real shaver, Jack. Guess that's why you're here." As he spoke, he wadded the paper into a ball and playfully tossed it into Jack's lap.

Jack laughed. "No hard feelings, Tom. I just wanted to get that out of the way. I guess you missed that class."

"Never was much of a student," he said. "I prefer workin' with my hands."

Jack wondered if Tom Braedon was his real name. It seemed to fit the bronzed, sun-creased face. "Where are you from?"

Braedon shifted in his chair. "I was born in Nebraska. But, I moved to Denver. You?"

"I'm from Las Vegas..." Jack let that sink in. Vegas was an unknown two-bit town in 1934, but in the future, it was just a few miles from the seat of government.

Tom smiled. "I get it. Believe me, I get it. Sorry about the tail. But, ya' know, orders are orders."

Jack lit another cigarette, took his time, and blew the smoke into the air. "Checking up on me?"

"Nothin' to worry about. I've got another assignment, but I was asked to report on you."

"Report what?"

"Nothin' serious. The home office just wanted me to check the fence-line...make sure that everything was goin' according to Hoyle."

Jack nodded. "Nebraska...I'd guess it was pretty quiet there when you were growing up."

"Yep. The family had a small ranch. I liked workin' the ranch, but that dried up. Parents passed on. I gave it up. Too much work—too little reward. It was a dyin' business."

"Where did you land?" Jack probed for verification.

"Here?"

"Right."

"Same place you did."

Jack waited.

"Bethesda."

Jack nodded again. Satisfied he knew who he was facing, he snuffed out his cigarette and leaned back. "OK, Tom. Where do we go from here?"

Braedon relaxed. "Jack, I don't have a dog in this fight," he wagged his head back and forth, widened his eyes, and his voice took on an apologetic tone. "And I'm just readin' between the lines. No one checks with me for my opinion. But, some folks are scratchin' their heads back home. There's been a bit of temporal disruption, if you know what I mean. This whole Roosevelt thing is making them nervous."

"And they said I'm responsible?" Jack leaned back and frowned.

Braedon shook his head. He leaned forward. "No. That's not it. Listen, Jack, we're fellow travelers. You've been around. Nobody trusts anyone at the home office. But let's face it, everyone knows it doesn't take much to mess with the future. That 'butterfly effect' story is B.S., but things do happen. I hear that before you got here, things were shaping up differently. Another pattern. A whole different state of affairs. We never did get martial law. And then there was a real election and everything."

"I'm aware," Jack said with an air of resignation. "Not much to be done with that."

The time-cop continued. His drawl increased as he talked, something that Jack liked. Braedon was comfortable now.

"Then the whole Miami deal. I guess that went south when some woman jostled the arm of the shooter. What's his name? Zangar or whatever?"

"Zangara."

"Right," said Braedon. "Well, that's what happens when you got a midget hitman standing on a folding chair."

"I read the details in the newspapers. I was there," said Jack. "But it was night. The only light in the place was on FDR and the stage. It was tough to follow. But I'll tell you what I think. I think someone sent the wrong guy to do the deed. End of story."

"Makes sense to me," said Braedon. "I've got no idea what the little guy was up to. All I know is that *The History* had one of those bullets flying into Franklin Roosevelt's head. That cowboy, Gardener should be drivin' the wagon train now."

"Garner. Vice President John Nance Garner," said Jack.

"Right. That's the guy. Whatever." Braedon lit a cigarette. "As I said…" he held the lit match while he made his point, "doesn't take much to mess with things." He blew out the match with a puff of smoke and tossed it into the ashtray. "But anyway, I was just told to keep an eye out for you. Nothin' to do with this Roosevelt thing."

"That's more information than I got."

"Don't blame me. Trust me, Jack. This is all new to me. I was supposed to check on you. You've been here a long time, I guess. Too much time in the field makes them nervous. Now, I can see why." He smiled.

"Why?"

"I saw that pretty gal you've got with you now. As I said, I don't blame ya'. A man's got needs. We had the same drill. We're supposed to avoid that extracurricular stuff."

Jack cocked his head and asked, "Is that what you do?"

Braedon laughed. "Jack, this is only my third assignment. None of them longer than a month. Not some two years like you. You know how long I lasted without a little girly action?"

"Tell me."

"First trip. Forty-six hours. Next one…a week." He grimaced. "And so far, this time…I've been a good boy. Personally, I think it's expecting too much out of a man. We are human. I mean away from home. All alone. And a whole lot of beautiful women just waiting for guys like us."

"They are tempting," Jack smiled and rolled his eyes.

"And another thing. I'm not pissed at all about you makin' me."

"I'm sure, if the roles were reversed, you would have done the same," said Jack trying to sound sincere.

He smiled. "That's how they train us. Right? They gotta' figure that might happen."

Jack nodded. "So, your assignment here doesn't involve me?"

He shook his head. "No. I did my job. I got the picture. I'll give the home office a head's up, and that will be that. I've got real work waitin' to be done."

"Does our work overlap?" asked Jack.

The man rubbed his chin with his thumb and forefinger knuckle. "You've got an inside job. Right? What's your game again?"

"I'm a troubleshooter for Mrs. Roosevelt. I report to her and the home office and take orders."

Braedon thought for a moment. "Do you ever work for her husband? Ever talk to him?"

"No. I doubt I ever will."

"Do you ever go to the White House?" His pitch rose in mock excitement.

Jack smiled. "Sure. That'll happen." He chuckled. "But what's the worry? Mrs. Roosevelt seems like a decent person. Who knows? Maybe her husband would be good for the future. These presidential elections are revolving doors. Politicians come, and they go."

Braedon's smile disappeared. "It's been that way. But this guy FDR seems to be takin' himself seriously. Fact is, Jack, I've been told he's a dangerous player. He's got this 'state of emergency' going and his Executive Orders, his 'Brains Trust,' and his 'New Deal.' He's out of control. The home office doesn't want any expansion of power in the Executive branch. It's not manageable. The Congress is full of quackin' ducks on the pond, swimmin' around goin' nowhere. And the Supreme Court...they're all tied up just keepin' the status quo. But this guy Roosevelt, he's a giant loose cannon. That's what they say. But anyway, I know my job. I don't think I'm givin' up any state secrets to say that you and I shouldn't cross paths. I'll be out of here by the end of the month."

A party of two men and two women drifted out of the bar and headed toward them. They sat nearby. They were loud, and they didn't care. Quickly, privacy ended.

Braedon snuffed out his cigarette, grabbed his hat,

and stood.

Jack looked up at the towering man thinking he was one big cowboy.

Tom Braedon adjusted his hat with two hands and squared his jaw. Looking down at Jack, he proclaimed, "I've gotta' go. But you oughta' make a phone call. Get that pretty gal of yours to come up for a drink. The evening's still young." He smiled. "You're a lucky guy. Hell, maybe I'll get lucky too. We can hope. See ya', Jack."

As he turned away, Jack tossed him a hint, "One more thing, Tom..."

"What's that?"

"I'd lose the hat," he said with a smile. "Buy something more conventional if you want to blend in."

Braedon gripped the brim of his hat and nodded. "I'll think about that, Jack. Thanks for the tip."

Travers waved goodbye and watched him lope away like a lonesome wayward horse. He wandered into the elevator and disappeared. Jack now knew that Tom Braedon was MOM's man in D.C. He wasn't buying Braedon's good ol' boy demeanor. As a time-cop, he knew Braedon was one they call a 'fixer.' He was there to make sure there were no hiccups in history. Everyone in the future and many people in the present wanted FDR to be put out to pasture. Braedon was here to make sure that happened.

-Chapter IX-

The Surprise

Dr. Currant, Ethan, and Zak were getting restless and itching to do something. They knew they had to keep FDR from falling from power in eleven days. But as they sat in their hotel room, ruminating about their next move, they started to get on each other's nerves. Their conversations became circular. Their minds struggled with the multitude of possibilities. Ideas flowed back and forth like an alternating electrical current, unbridled energy waiting to be tapped. Time travel acted like a powerful stimulant drug, immersion in another world of time and place, feeling both familiar and strange, created an exciting, euphoric, and wild internal buzz. The time travelers felt all-powerful and powerless at the same time. But knowing the future and determining a sensible method of changing future events required ingenuity, restraint, and wisdom.

Ethan did not lack the intelligence to approach the problem, but patience and stillness did not come naturally to him. He would admit his intensity and drive were best tempered by the intuition of Zak, the wisdom of Currant, the depth of Emma, and the intelligence analysis of Jack Travers. They were now a team working toward the same goal to keep Franklin Roosevelt in office. He and Emma had kept the dream alive. The twins might differ regarding the direction of their personal futures, but they were totally in sync with the belief that saving FDR would save the world from a dismal, oppressive, dystopic future.

The three men were dressed and ready to go. Currant was on his third coffee for the day and worked on his second cigarette. Zak read the newspaper, and Ethan stood before him, frozen as he gazed absentmindedly at the lead story: *Congressional Committee Battles*. Zak raised the paper. Ethan spotted another front-page article: *President Returns From Fishing Trip,* and grabbed the news out of Zak's hands.

Zak reacted with a "W*hat's up?*" gesture.

Ethan quickly read the article. "Listen up, guys. FDR is coming back from another fishing trip today. Remember the last time he went fishing? We were in Miami. Bullets were flying. Not a good time. Well, he's been on a fishing trip on his millionaire buddy Vincent Astor's yacht for the last two weeks." He read the article. "The *Nourmahal.* Wow! Two hundred sixty-three feet long. Crew of fifty men. Now that's some kind of fishing boat."

"What's your point?" asked Currant.

"My point is that we have to get going. It's April 13th. We've gotta' move. FDR is scheduled to return this morning from Florida. Coming in at Union Station. Why don't we go there? We can check him out. Maybe get an idea of his security. Heck, I never even got to see him in Miami."

Zak gave Ethan a sympathetic look.

Ethan flashed back to that night in the crowd over a year ago when his new girlfriend was shot and killed. The crowd went crazy; FDR was almost assassinated, and Mayor Cermak was hit. Zangara, the 'lone assassin,' was nearly ripped to pieces by the crowd. A wave of emotions rolled over Ethan and then quickly receded.

"Are you OK, Ethan? asked Currant.

Ethan paused for a moment. "No problem. What do you think?"

Zak signed, *"I agree. Let's get out of here. We're going nuts sitting around anyway."*

As they walked rapidly through the hotel lobby, A.C. Currant commented, "I remember something DuFour told me about FDR and this fishing trip."

"What?" asked Ethan.

Currant looked around. Strangers surrounded them. "I'll tell you in the cab," he said quietly.

The three men rode in the back seat of the taxi heading to Union Station. Currant spoke in hushed tones, constantly checking for a reaction from the driver. "DuFour said that there were rumors of other medical problems. The story came out after the big baseball game newsreel flap."

"About what?" asked Ethan.

"Not about his legs. About that mole on his forehead. Have you seen it? It's on the left side."

Ethan thought. "I've seen it in the photos. It's like a brown blob."

Zak put his finger to his head to identify the exact location above the left eye.

"Right," said Currant. "Well, there were rumors that this was a cancerous melanoma. The speculation was that he was taken ill on this fishing trip. That the trip was extended from a week to two weeks. And that he was even operated on aboard that yacht."

"Wow. Is any of that true?" Ethan asked.

"We'll get a look at him today. Maybe it will be evident," replied Currant.

Ethan looked ahead. As they neared the station, traffic was building. "What else?"

"According to the rumors flying around the nation," said Currant. "Some surgery was attempted. And radiation treatment. There was serious hemorrhaging. He was very ill. So ill that his sons were called in, and possibly blood transfusions were required."

Ethan nodded. "Fuel to the fire for all those calling for his immediate stand-down."

"Right."

"*Well, there's not much we can do about that,*" signed Zak.

Currant nodded.

"I don't believe it," said Ethan. "There was a photo in today's newspaper. It showed him on the yacht. I think at least one of his sons was in the photo. FDR appeared to be holding court with about ten men. He looked fine in the photo."

"The man is a consummate actor," said Currant. "He will never reveal anything about his health other than saying he's in great shape."

The taxi entered the crowded train station parking lot. In the distance, near the entrance to the station, they saw a Marine Corps brass band assembling.

"We'll get out here," said Currant. The driver pulled to a stop. Currant paid the man, and the three travelers quickly moved toward the crowd at the entrance. They couldn't get too close, but thanks to Ethan's height, he could see over the heads of those in front. They waited. Then they sensed something was happening. As the scene unfolded, Ethan reported the details to Zak and Currant. The crowd began to sputter and rumble, and the band played 'Hail to the Chief.' People shifted and swayed. Heat and excitement rose from the crowd. The citizens of the American empire awaited their hero, Franklin Delano Roosevelt, the great savior.

Later Ethan had read that over two hundred congressmen and thirty senators attended. Looking at the crowd before him, he discerned a group of finely dressed men standing at the station entrance on the stairs. They looked important. The poor and the rich, the weak and the powerful, Democrats and Republicans had all turned out to welcome home the President. Ethan sensed they needed him and that even his short two-week sojourn had increased the tension and fear among the people. The Great Depression caused the public to think differently about life. It was a solemn and scary time. Strong leaders were stepping up to claim their crowns in Europe and in the United States. Ethan knew in his heart that Franklin Roosevelt was the right leader for the country. He was a man of supreme confidence, a man of wealth and family nobility, yet he was also a man of the people.

"He's coming," said Ethan. "They're clearing the way for his car." It reminded Ethan of Roosevelt's arrival in Bayfront Park in Miami just before the shots were fired. The band played a new song, 'Happy Days are Here Again,' and the crowd cheered. It was obvious that the people loved their leader. Ethan spotted the center of attraction in the back seat of the open-topped car. If

Roosevelt was sick, he was a good actor. He smiled broadly and waved. The car pulled up and stopped. Someone placed a large microphone in front of him. His voice was clear and strong.

He opened with a brief commentary about the latest committee battle in Congress. The newspapers had reported that some believed the New Deal program was of communist inspiration. Of course, on the other side, the Democrats were saying all of these attacks were coming from dangerous fascists. But as he spoke, FDR joked about all of the name callings. "I gather also that both houses of Congress have been having a wonderful time in my absence." The audience laughed. FDR showed his teeth with his famous smile and continued finishing with a statement directed at Congress, "I did have a wonderful holiday, and I have come back with all sorts of new lessons which I learned from the barracuda and sharks. I am a tough guy. So, if you will come down and see me as often as you possibly can, I will teach you some of the stunts I learned."

The crowd laughed and bubbled over with excitement and applause. Ethan speculated that FDR could simply read from a telephone book, and people would love it. The microphone was removed, and the car moved on. FDR flashed his trademark smile, waved, and jutted his chin for effect. And in a few minutes, he and his entourage were on their way to the White House. Ethan looked around as the crowd detached themselves from the event. One person caught his eye. He was a tall man wearing a tan cowboy hat. For a brief moment, the eyes of these two tall men scanning the area above the crowd locked on each other, then moved on.

Ethan looked down at his friends. "That's it, guys. Did you get a look?"

"Right," said Currant. "The only radiation I saw was that from the sun. FDR looked tanned and fit."

They decided to walk back to the Mayflower Hotel, stopping for lunch on the way. Zak needed a 1930s hamburger fix, and they found the perfect joint to assuage his cravings.

Later that afternoon, they relaxed in their suite back at the hotel. "This trip must be costing you a fortune, A.C.," said Ethan.

Currant laughed. "Don't worry. They only take cash here. And that's one thing I have plenty of."

"No gold coins, I hope," said Ethan.

A.C. thought for a moment. "The law says I could have a hundred dollars in gold coins. That will buy a whole lot of hamburgers. But I'm patriotic. I only use paper money. And I have plenty of that from my racetrack winnings last year." He laughed. "You know I was very good at picking the winners. I'm quite the handicapper."

"You are. Especially when you can reverse engineer the newspaper reports of all the winning horses," signed Zak.

Currant shrugged his shoulders. "Every gambler needs an edge. Mine is knowing history before it happens."

"Which reminds me. I want to check that newspaper you ripped out of my hands this morning."

Ethan picked up the paper from the coffee table and tossed it at Zak. "Reading up on Heinie Manush?" he asked.

"He's my man. We'll get to see him in action on opening day." Zak poured himself into the sports section of the paper.

"Let's hope that's all the action on that day," said Ethan.

"Not to worry. We've still got almost a couple of weeks to rewrite history," said Currant. "But time is running out. And we don't know much about anything. We could try and reach Emma by phone. That's still an option. Right?"

"I think so. Jack only said she shouldn't meet with us in person. I think..."

Zak rose to his feet and held up the sports section. He pointed to the headline of the lead article. *"Senator's Home Opener. Can They Repeat?".*

Ethan snatched the newspaper and read it aloud. *"The*

new season is coming for Joe Cronin's Washington Senators. Can they repeat the success of 1933 and win the American League pennant again? Fans will get their first opportunity to see this year's team this Monday, April 16th, at Griffith Stadium when our boys...."

"Whoa!" exclaimed A.C. Currant. "Read that again."

Ethan scanned the text. He was too stunned to reread it. "What the heck. This can't be right."

The three men read and reread the newspaper. They checked the dates. They read all the stories about the upcoming home opener and were confused, bewildered, and concerned.

"Bad news, fellows. The game will be played three days from now. Not on the twenty-fourth. DuFour or *The History* got it all wrong."

"We're screwed," signed Zak. *"Eso Que Ni Que."*

"Worse than that, FDR is screwed," said Ethan as he looked up at the ceiling, searching for an answer. "We have to get the word out. Somehow. We're never going to be able to figure out a plan of action. We have no idea why he fell. Maybe it just happened. Maybe something was wrong with the braces. Maybe someone pushed him."

"Nobody pushed him, Ethan," said Currant. "We all saw the newsreel movie. Roosevelt tossed out the game ball, and in the process, he fell. All of us agree that his right leg seemed to give. It caved in. And slowly he fell...stone cold like a tree. It's possible there was something wrong with his leg braces, but he had fallen in public before."

"Not like this," said Ethan.

"We don't know. Who knows? The man is physically unstable. Once he is wearing those braces and standing, he's balancing like a hundred-pound weight teetering on two sticks. Anything could happen. He is a master magician creating the illusion that his legs are supporting and propelling him. But in reality, they are just dead weight. They cannot move. They can only be manipulated to simulate walking."

"So, what are you saying?" asked Ethan. "We can't

save him?"

Currant ran his hands through his hair. "I'm saying we know nothing. We can't even warn him without showing our hand. What are we going to say? Be careful, Mr. President; you might fall?" Current flopped down onto the sofa. "I think we should toss this whole deal back to Jack. He can talk with Mrs. Roosevelt. He can tell her to have the braces double-checked. And ask her to have her husband take extra precautions. Maybe have someone standing next to him. Maybe toss the ball out from a sitting position. I don't know. But I do know that we don't have enough time for this. If we had more time, we could discover more about his braces. Maybe there's something obvious. But maybe FDR is just weak from radiation treatments and surgery on the yacht. If any of that is true...." He trailed off and sunk deeper into the soft sofa cushions.

Exasperated, Ethan blew out a blast of air. "I don't care. I'm going to see Emma."

"*But she told us to stay away. Telephone calls only,*" signed Zak.

"That was before. When we had time to be cautious. Emma needs to know." He grabbed the newspaper's sports section, threw on his jacket, and opened the door. "I've got to talk it out with her and Jack. Call her. Tell her I'll be there in fifteen minutes." He slammed the door as he left.

"You forgot your hat," Currant muttered as he held Ethan's fedora.

Zak shook his head and signed. "*I've got a bad feeling about this.*"

-Chapter X-

Running Out of Time

Ethan flagged down a cab in front of the hotel. He offered the driver an extra dollar for a speedy trip, and the man earned his money. Fifteen minutes later, the cab slid to a stop; Ethan popped out and ran toward Jack's apartment. He hoped Currant had made the call to Emma and forewarned her. She would not be pleased to see him. As usual, he was moving headfirst into action and paying no heed to Jack's instructions. He knocked on the entry door. When his sister opened it, he could tell he was in for a lecture. Emma wore an Asian kimono. Her hair was in a state of disarray. "Sorry about the intrusion, Emma," he mumbled.

"Get in here."

He entered, and she quickly closed the door. He surmised this was not a good time for visitors. The Murphy bed was down, and Jack was sitting on its edge. He wore a bathrobe. Ethan took a deep breath. "Did Dr. Currant call you?"

"Yes, he called," she said.

Ethan could tell his sister was perturbed. She stood before him with her hands on her hips.

Meanwhile, Jack got up and looked out the bay window at the street.

"I wish you would think a little bit before you go into a wild frenzy," she said.

Ethan swallowed. "I wouldn't call it a wild frenzy. I'd say it was an appropriate reaction to what we learned today."

"Which is?"

Ethan mentally moved off Emma's rant and attacked the problem. "Look. We just found out that the opening day baseball game is scheduled for Monday, April 16th, not April 24th." She looked stunned. He had her attention now.

"How can that be? Professor DuFour wouldn't get that wrong," she said.

Ethan pulled the newspaper from his jacket pocket. "Here. Look at this. The game is on Monday." He pointed to the article, and she grabbed the paper from him.

"Is this right, Jack?"

"I don't know, honey. I don't follow baseball. But if it's in black and white in the paper, I think you can assume that's the date."

"We have to do something. And fast." She thought for a moment and looked at Ethan. "Sorry I yelled at you, but Jack is concerned that he's being followed by another time-cop. He doesn't want them to make the connection between you and us."

"That's OK," he said. "Not important. What's important is that we must warn the President." He turned to Jack. "Can you help?"

Jack tightened his robe. "Pull up a chair, Ethan. Let's talk."

Ethan sat in the desk chair while Emma and Jack sat on the edge of the bed.

"I know the story. Emma has run it by me several times. The entire event boils down to Mr. Roosevelt losing his balance and falling." Before continuing, he lowered his head and rubbed his forefinger and thumb across his mustache. "But we don't know why he lost his balance."

"True, but he will," said Ethan. "Dr. Currant says you should talk to Mrs. Roosevelt and have her tell her husband."

"Tell him what?" Jack asked quietly.

"Tell him..." Ethan trailed off, not knowing where to go next.

"Can I tell her that her husband will fall on Monday? And the whole world will see it. And the nation will lose faith in him as a leader because he appears to be a helpless cripple."

"Why not?"

"Ethan, we can't do that. The first question she'll ask

is how would you possibly know that?" said Emma.

"Also, I just don't have that kind of access to her. She calls me when she wants to meet. I don't call her," said Jack.

"So, where are we?" asked Ethan.

Jack thought. "Maybe I could set up an emergency meeting with her if I tie it all to one of my current projects with her."

"How's that?"

"I'm working on redirecting a plot to undermine FDR sponsored by a sector of the rich, powerful, and elite. These people have no use for President Roosevelt. They see him as the next Stalin. Afraid he is going to confiscate all their wealth and property. They want him out."

"What's their plan?" asked Ethan.

Jack got up from the bed. "Truth is, I'm not very comfortable bringing you into this. So far, I've maintained a low profile. But I've been successful in getting the bad guys moving in a direction which I believe will fail."

Ethan made a face. "Listen, Jack. We're all in this together. Emma says you're on our side. Is she mistaken?"

Jack walked over to the kitchen counter and poured himself a drink. He held up his glass. "Anyone else?" Emma shook her head.

"Not a big drinker, Jack. What about it? Are you working one hundred percent to keep the man in the White House?"

Jack took a sip of whiskey and replied. "I'm in all the way, Ethan. Just like you. But I like my job, and I work for Mrs. Roosevelt. She calls the shots, and I like to keep things on a 'need to know' basis."

"Well, I think she needs to know, Jack. I assume she knows that people are plotting against her husband. Right?"

"That's a given. There are plenty of people out to get him. This thing I'm onto goes much higher than someone tripping the President. Bigger players. Great forces."

"Yeah. I get it. You're shaping the forces of history. And

Zak, Currant, and I are just here to hold FDR's hand."
Ethan leaned back in the chair. "You seem to forget the
role Dr. Currant played in Miami. You were just there to
observe. Then you found another plot on top of the one
you were watching. Then you needed help. And you got it,
right?"

Jack Travers leaned against the counter, sipping
slowly as if the whiskey was filling his head with ideas.
He smiled at Ethan. "You're correct, my friend. The
difference was that it was my plan. I'm accustomed to
working alone. It's a way of staying alive." He tipped his
glass in the direction of Emma. "If it weren't for your
sister, I wouldn't be talking to you today. The fewer
moving parts, the less chance the machine will break
down."

"And you see me like a monkey wrench waiting to be
tossed into the gears?" Ethan folded his arms in front of
him and waited for an answer.

Jack set the glass down. "For example. You're here.
You're not supposed to be here. Now you may have been
spotted by my friend with the cowboy hat. If that's the
case, he'll connect the three of us and our attempt to stop
'Operation Opening Day'. If such a thing exists. Then it
will become part of my world. Right now, I don't think he
suspects anything. But what if he starts watching you?
He's a trained agent. He knows I'm a 'TT.' Maybe he'll
figure out that you're one. We're all done for if that gets
back to the home office. That's why I like
compartmentalization. That's why you shouldn't be here."

"I get it," said Ethan, but I'm here now."

"This is true," said Jack. "Let me think." He gazed out
the window at the fading light.

Ethan was impatient. He stood. "So...?"

"Well. I'm willing to gamble. I'll try to see Mrs. R
tonight. I'll tell her that I've come across some information
that makes me believe the anti-Roosevelt forces may try
to speed up the demise of her husband. That they may
want to embarrass him. I'll tell her to ensure their son
Jimmy is by his side. The President can hold his son's

arm. There's nothing unusual about this. If that's the case, even if he falls, he can catch himself. He has a powerful upper body."

"Jack, in the videos I've seen, Jimmy is not next to him. FDR stands alone, holding on to the handrail in front of him."

"OK, I get it. Let me talk to Mrs. Roosevelt. Now, I want you out of here. The backway. You should go now."

Ethan nodded.

Emma got up and hugged her brother. "Sorry, Ethan. Friends?"

"Yep," he replied. Like a big kid just scolded, he dropped his head and followed Jack to the rear exit, which led to a stairway and ultimately out of the building. He didn't mention that he had seen a tall man wearing a cowboy hat that morning at the train station. But, he was now sure that Jack was telling the truth about the other time-cop. They would have to be careful.

It was after midnight in the early morning of April 14, 1934. Jack had called the White House and left a message for Mrs. Roosevelt to call him. About ten o'clock, he received a call. After a brief conversation, she agreed to meet him at a friend's home in Georgetown. Travers parked his car about two blocks from his destination. He walked through the old neighborhood filled with mansions and high-end row houses. There was no automobile traffic. Large elms lined the quiet and protected residences that belonged to the money in Washington. In a few minutes, he found the house number and approached the imposing three-story Georgian home where a man was waiting at the front door. He presented his identification to the Secret Service agent. The agent used his penlight to scan it. Satisfied, he escorted Travers into the home.

Their footsteps echoed off the marble entry. It was a large home with elegant formal furnishings, plenty of plaster detailing, and fine woodwork with traditional paintings hanging on the walls. If there was anyone home, they were not evident. He didn't travel far to reach his destination. As the agent opened a door for him, he entered a large, heavily-paneled study. A wall of books filled one end, and a large window bay capped the other. Heavy curtains shut off views into the room. In front of the windows, two large period sofas and a couple of armchairs surrounded a low table. Eleanor Roosevelt sat with her back to him. The agent closed the door loud enough to announce his departure. Jack walked up to her and stood nearby. He greeted her with a simple "Mrs. Roosevelt" and sat opposite her on the other sofa. "Let me start with my apologies for requesting this meeting, but I believe it is important," he said.

"I'm sure you do," she said. "Let's get right to the point. As you know, it is difficult for me to move out of the spotlight, even for a brief period. According to the White House log, I am on a train traveling to Herkimer, New York. I'm afraid I wasn't very creative, but that is one of the shortcomings of this kind of emergency meeting."

"I understand, and I appreciate how difficult your situation is. But..." He paused. "The President may be in danger."

"Is this related to your General Butler assignment?" she asked.

Jack shifted in his chair. "To be honest, I can't be certain. You know I'm monitoring those people from a distance, so I do not have real-time information. But we know they are planning something on a macro scale. Their intent is clear. They want to either remove the President from office or minimize his power. I believe there are big players behind this whole Butler thing. But they are moving slowly, so I'm guessing this is a backup plan."

"What kind of plan?"

To relieve his tension, Jack breathed in heavily through his nose. "Something like last year in Miami."

She didn't respond. She inhaled deeply and gazed blankly into the distance while placing both hands on her cheeks. Then she drew them together over her mouth, her hands finally resting in a prayer position. "When?" she asked quietly.

"Very soon. Two days from now. At the ballgame."

"I was afraid of this. How do you know?"

"It is better that I don't tell you. And I should say that I don't have any information that suggests a physical attack on the President. I think they know that would be too obvious after the Zangara incident. Also, the President's security is much better now that he is in office."

"Jack, I am confused. What then is the attack?"

He stumbled. "The information I have is credible...but sketchy. I'm told that the President will suffer a fall at the ballgame. It will be a serious fall. But it will cause him only minor physical damage."

She looked relieved. Her cheeks regained color, and her eyes brightened.

"Franklin has fallen before. The fact that this can happen is always on his mind. But on those few occasions where something has gone wrong, he has recovered physically, mentally, and, I guess I would say, politically. But I think I see where this is headed. They are out to embarrass the President."

"That is what I believe."

"Should we warn the security people?"

"As far as I can tell, there is nothing they could do, and I don't want to compromise my sources. Do you understand?"

She paused. "Then how can we protect Franklin?"

"This attack is scheduled for the opening day ceremonies. At the tossing out of the first pitch...."

She interrupted. "There is no way we can stop him from doing that. He loves baseball and the opportunity to bask in the limelight. There is nothing more American than opening day at the ballpark. It allows him to display his strength and vigor by tossing that ball. It's tradition. He is going to do it. I am certain."

Jack nodded. "That's fine. I assumed that. However, that is the moment...when all the cameras are focused on him...when every eye in the stadium is looking at him...that is when they want him to go down."

"Are you certain?"

"I'm certain enough to be here with you at one in the morning talking about it. Yes, it's a serious threat. Again, to the point. If the President is going to fall, it will happen at that moment. There are several things that we can do. We can ask him to have your son Jimmy stand by his side. Jimmy can steady him as he throws and stop him from falling."

She shook her head. "Franklin and I have talked about this. That is not in his plan. He wants to grab the rail before him. Rise. Stabilize his legs. And brace himself on the railing with his left hand and throw with the other. He calls it triangulation. Once he has those three points established, he is like a rock. You know he is powerful, and his grip on the railing will be intense. He has done this before without a problem. I can't see why this time would be any different. You don't think someone will push him, do you?"

"No," said Jack, "that would be too obvious. "The answer may be in the braces he wears. If someone toyed with the locking mechanisms of the braces, they could fail, and he would fall."

"Strange, you should mention that." The pitch of her voice rose.

"Why?"

"He's getting new braces. Special lightweight braces. I think they're aluminum. They will be half the weight of the old ones."

"Does he have them now?"

"No. They haven't arrived. But he's expecting them soon. Next week sometime. This is an exciting thing for him."

"Well, you can't let him use them on Monday. They must be carefully inspected."

She scoffed. "Franklin will do what he wants to do. He is no fool when it comes to his braces. He has an engineering mind, you know. I could not tell him. Nor would I know if there was a problem."

"What about his valet?"

"Irvin? He's a wonderful man."

"Can you ask him to scrutinize the old braces on the day of the game? Particularly the locking devices."

"Yes, I'm sure it is part of his morning routine, but I'll have him do that without alarming anyone. I don't want to mention it to Franklin. It might affect his behavior, and that wouldn't be good. He has spent years perfecting his walking, standing, and sitting habits. The whole thing is quite a beautiful ballet of movements and procedures. Now, he does it flawlessly and with an air of nonchalance. I don't want to make him self-conscious. That would only make things worse."

"And your son Jimmy?"

She cocked her head to the side before looking back at Jack. "I will...I will ask him to stay near Franklin's side during the ceremony. I can advise him without raising any questions, but I assure you that Franklin will not be holding on to his arm."

"And these new braces. Who's making them?"

"I don't know the name of the manufacturer. I guess I could find out. I think it is someone in New York...a new supplier. NRA approved according to that man General Smith. He convinced Franklin that he couldn't use the previous supplier because that firm was not registered with the government."

"No Blue Eagle?"

"I guess not," she said. "Although, I don't like or listen to most of what the General says. He drinks too much and talks too loudly." She looked at her watch. "I must be going soon."

"Right. I understand. Thank you for this meeting. As soon as possible, please send me a message informing me of the manufacturer and the scheduled delivery date of the new braces. If they arrive before the game, do not let the President wear them to the game. I'm sorry to be so dogmatic about this, but it is critical."

"If I have to hide them. I will do that. He won't be wearing them to the game. And I will have his current braces inspected carefully by his valet, Mr. McDuffie. I trust him completely."

"All right," said Jack. "I'll be leaving. And don't worry. I think this is under control." He paused and thought for a moment. "If the valet does find something amiss with the existing braces, something that would force the President to use the new braces, please do not let it happen. Cancel his appearance at the game. Say the President's ill or some excuse. But our best plan is to inspect the old braces carefully and use them."

"I understand. And Jack, thank you."

He left her sitting in the room. The Secret Service agent escorted him out of the house. The door closed behind him, and the sound rattled the evening. The sky was clear, the night air was cool, and Washington was asleep.

Everyone waited. Nothing else could be done. So far as Ethan knew, Jack had made his pitch to Mrs. Roosevelt. To pass the time, Zak, Currant, and Ethan went sightseeing. Saturday passed uneventfully. By Sunday afternoon, Ethan could not stand the inactivity. He went to Griffith Stadium to buy tickets for the upcoming game. He wanted seats above the infield, but none were available. Earlier that morning, Zak had revealed that he had brought his *Voicenator*. Having seen many available young women, he no longer wished to be socially hamstrung. Against the advice of Ethan and Dr. Currant, he was out on his own, wearing the device concealed by the collar of his turtleneck sweater. A.C. Currant was visiting the Smithsonian Museum. For him, a scientist, this was the perfect way to spend the day.

At breakfast in the hotel coffee shop the next day, Monday, April 16, 1934, opening day for all baseball fans in Washington, D.C., three apprehensive time travelers sat at a table by the window, nibbled at their food, and discussed the state of their new world. Outside, the people of Washington hustled about, unaware of the potential disaster soon to occur. Heavy gray clouds drifted across the sky. Currant read a neatly folded newspaper highlighting the news to pass the time. Adolph Hitler was busy getting legislation passed in Germany, creating a new family code. Only 'racially pure' couples would be permitted to marry. And on the flip side, only childless married couples would be allowed to divorce. Hitler intended to provide a government bonus for those with more than two children. These ten-dollar monthly bonus payments would be financed from government savings produced by an active forced-sterilization program.

"Neat and tidy," noted Zak. His artificial voice was clear and accurate. Obviously, he was enjoying his renewed vocal skills.

Currant also reported that Congress was still investigating whether the Roosevelt administration had hidden within communist agents working to prepare the country for a Soviet-style *coup*. It was business as usual in Washington.

"What about the sports section?" asked Ethan.

Currant moved to the back of the paper, scanned the headline, and read it aloud: "*FDR to toss out the first pitch, twenty-five thousand fans expected to see the classic home opener.*"

Ethan checked his watch: 11:30. "Let's go back to the room and see if we can pick up the game on the radio." Zak took one last gulp of coffee, Currant signed for the bill, and they ventured upstairs to their room.

Ethan dialed the black knob on the old Philco cathedral radio, and after a few seconds, the signal arrived. Ethan didn't take long to locate the distinctive voice of the play-by-play announcer. "*This is Arch McDonald. Here today to bring you the home opener of the 1934 Washington Senators' season. We're in our WJSV radio booth atop Griffith Stadium, bringing you the play-by-play broadcast of the Senators against the Boston Red Sox. Maybe Mrs. Murphy will shine upon us today, but for the moment, we are stuck in low gear...waiting for the weather to break and the nation's number one sports fan,*

President Franklin Delano Roosevelt, to arrive. Mother Nature has taken over. The rain is falling continuously, and they are bringing out the tarp. And unfortunately, it looks like we'll have a rain delay. Will be back with the lineups and more, but while we're waiting, let's get in a word from our sponsor...."

The three men sat facing the radio listening to every word. A light rain began to fall outside their window, unnoticed by them. The rain turned into a thunderstorm pelting the windows in a few minutes and darkening the room. As Ethan gazed through the window, a white wall of water obscured his view down to the street.

After a series of commercial announcements, the sportscaster's voice returned. *"Welcome back, folks. Well, we're not so lucky today. The rain continues to fall like crazy. Unfortunately, we have received the announcement from Clark Griffith...the owner of the Senators...that this game has been called because of rain. I am told it has been rescheduled for next Tuesday, April 24th. The Senators will go on the road, and you can hear those games right here on WJSV...."*

Zak clicked off the radio, and the time travelers looked at each other. First, Zak snickered. Then they all slid into a tension-relieving laugh. There would be no opening day Presidential pitch today. They now knew they could go back to work to save FDR.

LOG of Zak Newman
April 17, 1934 (local time): 22:12 (Day 9 of time travel)

Well, for the moment, FDR is safe and sound in his White House bed. The rain has stopped, but the baseball game won't happen for a whole week. So, we have some time. After much discussion, we are going to Plan B. We know the new braces are coming. We got word from Jack. He told us the name and address of the manufacturer. It's someplace in New York City called Long Island City. We also know that a thorough inspection of FDR's existing braces was made this morning by his valet. Nothing is amiss. Nothing is new. No signs of tampering. Via the Jack connection, the valet has been told to keep a close eye on these. Currant is planning a trip. He's going to New York tomorrow and attempting to get a close-up view of the manufacturer and his equipment. Today, he put in a special order for stationary and business cards. I guess money is the root of all speed because he gave the printer a bonus for fast delivery. He also bought a portable typewriter machine. He's been practicing all day. Surprisingly he remembers how to operate the machine. I guess he took typing lessons in high school.

Today he sent a telegram to the brace manufacturer saying he would like to visit their factory for an inspection tour. He wants to get a look at FDR's new leg braces and also wants to find out the exact delivery date.

There's not too much Ethan and I can do while Currant is gone. We can't visit Emma. Jack has forbidden that. So, I guess we will go sightseeing. There's plenty to see in Washington. Maybe we'll run into some nice young women. Hopefully, Dr. Currant will be back no later than late Friday. That gives us four days before the postponed home opener. End 04-17-34

-Chapter XI-

Gabriel Blows His Horn

As A.C. Currant entered the shop, a small printing press pounded rhythmically in the background, and a strange aromatic blend of ink and cigar smoke floated in the air. The ambiance felt comfortable, even cozy, to Currant. Although he was born in the 1950s, everything in the shop reminded him of his childhood's simple and quiet days. Some old part of him longed for the comfort and innocence of a world now lost. For a few seconds, his mind floated aimlessly on the swirling seas of time. His reverie was interrupted by the print shop owner, who dropped a cardboard box on the counter and announced the completion of his work. "One hundred sheets finished, one hundred sheets blank, one hundred envelopes finished, and one hundred business cards. Take a look."

Currant did a quick examination of the man's work. It was pretty decent and would undoubtedly serve his needs: *Dr. Arthur C. Gabriel, Orthopedic Analyst, 728 Bridgewater Avenue, Portsmouth, New Hampshire.* There was even a little caduceus symbol imprinted on one side. Currant fingered one of the crisp, white business cards, gave it a serious look, and put it into his shirt pocket. "Very good," he said. "Very good."

"Great. That will be seven dollars seventy-five cents, Dr. Gabriel." The printer's tone was apologetic. As A.C. Currant removed his wallet to make payment, the man continued. "You know you could have got a whole lot more for just a couple of extra bucks."

Currant placed the exact amount on the counter and looked at the man. "Thank you, my friend. But I just ran short. This will be fine. And thanks for the speedy service."

The little bald man smiled. "Any time you're in town,

Doctor. We appreciate the business."

A.C. Currant grabbed the two boxes and walked out of the shop. A little bell at the top of the door gently announced his departure.

Once back at the hotel, he went directly to work. He was pleased Zak and Ethan were out. There would be no interruptions. He took off his coat and hat, tossed them on a bed, and then went to work on the Remington typewriter. Rolling in the sheet of stationery just as he did in Mrs. Fawcett's typing class back at Madison High School, he began to type out a letter to the Eastern Precision Metal Fabrications Company. The letter was backdated three days. The text reminded them of the telegram he had sent yesterday announcing his impending arrival. He thanked them in advance for the opportunity to view their orthopedic appliance manufacturing operation. He apologized for the short notice informing them that he was a medical equipment analyst and wanted to make the most of this business trip from New Hampshire to Washington. Usually, he would be satisfied to have one of their distributor's salespeople present their orthopedic product line, but this was a special inspection.   He explained that he was in Washington D.C. to meet with Senator Ferguson to discuss the needs of the veterans of the World War. He reminded them of the unfortunately large number of wounded soldiers requiring special appliances. Like a seasoned reporter, he pulled the letter out with a flourish, reviewed it, and signed it boldly with a fountain pen. Then he typed the address on an envelope, folded the letter, carefully slid it in, sealed it, and placed a three-cent, first-class stamp. "There you go. Doctor Gabriel is coming," he muttered.

The train ride from Washington to New York City was uneventful but exciting. Currant loved the steam, the whistleblowing, the rocking and rolling, and the unraveling of a scenic view of America's east coast in

1934. He was comfortable in this world of the past, and he didn't argue with Emma's decision to stay in this time. She and her man were enjoying life, each other, and making history. Sadly, comparing the future to the year 1934 was like comparing a cheap bottle of beer to a classic cut-glass tumbler filled with three fingers of Johnnie Walker Black. The former filled one's stomach. The latter filled one's soul. Since Currant had the advantage of sipping that drink while traveling today, the time passed quickly.

Soon the first signs of the heart of New York City appeared, and the train slid beneath the metropolis like a snake through wet grass. The train slowed and jerked to a stop. Currant grabbed his carryall and stepped onto the platform of the main concourse of Pennsylvania Station. Gazing at the underside of the roof structure, he was dazzled by the immense beauty of the delicate lacy steel fabrications that filtered the shafts of streaming daylight from the skylights and windows above.

He danced his way through the crowd and emerged from the cavernous building. Immediately he was overwhelmed by the beat of the city, its cacophony of sounds, rushing traffic, and brooding tall buildings. A quick cab ride brought him to the Lexington Hotel in mid-town Manhattan, where he checked in, went directly to his room, and called the orthopedic manufacturer. A lovely voice met his. "Eastern Precision Metal Fabrications..."

"That's a mouthful. Dr. Gabriel here. And may I ask who I have the pleasure of speaking with?"

There was a pause. "This is Mrs. Dougherty, Doctor. How may I help you?"

"Yes. Hello, Mrs. Dougherty. Did you receive my telegram?"

"Uh...we did, but...."

"I know. It's getting late in the day, but I'm sort of on my way. So..."

"Well, I understand. I have mentioned your request to Mr. Sullivan. It's a bit unusual. We don't get that many visitors or telegrams, for that matter."

"Not that many professionals are as diligent as I am. Anyway. Did you say I should stop by?"

"Could you make it tomorrow? Most everyone is gone now."

"I'll take the risk. As I said, I'm halfway there already."

"Well, if you are on your way. That's fine. But it is getting late. We close at four-thirty."

"I'll be there in a few minutes. By the way, I had a letter of introduction to your firm, but I forgot to put it into the box. Please, remind me if I forget again. And thank you, Mrs. Dougherty."

"You're welcome, Doctor. Goodbye."

Her tone was pleasant but businesslike. Currant couldn't assess her reaction, and he didn't want to annoy the gatekeeper. He would make a point of schmoozing her properly when he arrived. Knowing Eastern Precision was a small outfit, he suspected she might be someone who could facilitate his mission.

Currant hopped into a taxi. The driver made a right turn on 59th Street, crossed the river at Welfare Island, and arrived in an area of Long Island City filled with tight streets and warehouse buildings. The cab dropped Currant in front of a one-story yellow brick structure identified by a weathered bronze plaque mounted on the wall of its small entrance niche. Standing at the door, he took a deep breath, cleared his mind, and peered through the diamond-shaped, wire-glass window. It revealed a dimly lighted, tiny reception area without seating. The mottled green linoleum floor showed wear marks beneath the reception window; yellowed white paint peeled from the ceiling, and the plastered walls were finger-marked, nicked, and chipped. Eastern Precision people didn't expect to entertain many guests. As he entered, the two panes of the sliding glass reception window rattled against each other to announce his presence. The window snapped open. He quickly focused on a beautiful woman looking at him from behind a desk. He wondered why she was stranded in the wilderness of Long Island City.

She spoke, and her voice was even more interesting than it had been on the phone. "Dr. Gabriel?"

Entranced by her looks, he almost forgot who he was supposed to be. "Yes, yes. That I am." He reached into his pocket and passed her a business card through the window. Then he remembered the letter. "I never did get a chance to mail this to you. I'm sorry," he said as he handed it to her.

She accepted it with a smile. "I'll give this to Mr. Sullivan." She glanced briefly at her wristwatch.

It was a graceful, subtle move that Currant admired. In truth, he admired everything he saw. Mrs. Dougherty was maybe in her early forties, with raven-colored hair, fair skin, and...no ring on her finger. Currant soaked this in quickly. "It's late, isn't it? Probably too late for a visit. But I'm not sorry I made the trip." He smiled.

She gave him a little smirk-smile. Currant was pleased with this accidental encounter and determined to make the best of it. Chronologically he was 79 years old, but thanks to the miracles of modern science, he looked, sounded, and moved like a 1930s man in his early fifties. He tossed out the bait. "This may seem a little forward, but I'm traveling alone, and I hate eating alone. And..."

She rolled backward slightly in her chair. Then a fat, bald head popped out from a door behind her. The man said, "I'll be leaving in five minutes. You ready?"

She looked back. "I am."

"OK," The head retreated.

She turned back to look Currant in the eyes. He anticipated rejection, but her eyes seemed to welcome him. "I did say I was 'Mrs. Dougherty.'"

Currant pursed his lips. "I remember that now." His head dropped slightly.

"Well. It's true. But...I am a widow for quite some time now. And I do eat dinner every night...alone. So, I get it. And since you've been so nice about coming here and being sent away, I think that would be fine."

"So, we're on." He smiled. "That's great. I'm mid-town. At the Lexington Hotel. Could you meet me at the main restaurant at the hotel at...say seven o'clock? That would make my day."

She made a note on a pad on her desk and then stared at him for a few unsettling seconds without saying a word.

"What?"

"Just checking. A gal like me has to be cautious."

"And?"

"And you passed the test. See you then, Doctor Gabriel."

"Call me Arthur."

She smiled. "OK, Arthur. And I'm Margaret."

Upon returning to his hotel, A.C. Currant took a nap, a nip of whiskey, and a lazy bath. As he sat in the spacious, two-story lobby of the Lexington, he was pleased with himself. Tonight's dinner was his first special date of 1934. He delighted in meeting women from different eras. The last one had been with a sweet lady from Miami in 1933. He met her on one of the racetrack trips he used to finance his time travel excursions. Typically, and often, he preferred life in the late Fifties. Strictly for pleasure, he used his *TimeTravelle* machine to shoot back to Mystic Heights in the era of Elvis, big-finned automobiles, and A-bomb tests. Over time, he had established a detailed fictitious identity for himself as a traveling salesman for a laboratory equipment company supposedly located in Boston. He stayed in town regularly, spending evenings in the downtown hotel bar. He was familiar with the times and had no problem conversing with the natives about anything. He got to know several women. Of course, he would only stay one night. He would tell them he was leaving on the early morning train back to Boston. But in reality, he would sneak back to the top of the cliff overlooking Smuggler's Cove and time travel back to the present.

But Margaret was not one of his typical dates. For them, he only needed to provide a bit of charm and a good time. He suspected she swam in deeper waters. She was a widow, making him feel more responsible, respectful, and even a bit guilty. These were tough times, the 'Great Depression.' She appeared to be a hard-working, no-nonsense lady. He wasn't about to take advantage of her. He told himself he would just show her a good time, get to know her, pump her for information about Mr. Roosevelt's leg braces, and establish himself as someone she could trust. This trip would be wasted if he couldn't look closely at those new braces and didn't identify the scheduled delivery date.

With these thoughts in mind, he looked up, and Mrs. Dougherty passed through the revolving door into his view. She spotted him, smiled brightly, and he smiled back, admiring her. The receptionist had transformed herself from a plain-Jane warehouse worker to a handsome and stylish woman who carried herself with grace. He took her in—foot to head. Sensible high heels, silk stockings, a navy blue tailored skirt, a big-buttoned patterned jacket worn tight to the neck, and a white Peter Pan collar completed the thoughtful ensemble. It was all off-the-rack, but she wore it well.

"Margaret...you are looking exceptional."

"I've been told I clean up nicely," she said.

"That is the truth and then some. Any problem getting here?"

"Not at all. I hopped a streetcar to the trolley line, crossed over the river on the Queensboro Bridge, and it deposited me just up the street. I took a taxi from the station. I get over this way every so often. Mostly shopping at Christmas time."

Currant nodded. "Well, you seem to know your way around town. I'm very pleased that you could make it. Shall we...?" He offered his arm to her, and they walked as a couple into the restaurant.

They settled in over a round of drinks: a Scotch whiskey for him and a gin fizz for her. She gazed about the restaurant as if she was recording every detail. As he sipped his whiskey, she talked. He studied her. Fine-featured, smooth pale skin, bright blue eyes, and dark brown hair. Currant found her incredibly attractive. Only her hands revealed her age and history. Short nails, finger joints slightly knotted from hard work, and a tinge of red probably brought on by hand washing clothes and scrubbing floors. She caught him looking at her hands and slowly slid them off the table out of sight. She asked about his profession. Currant knew enough about orthopedics to sound knowledgeable about bones, muscles, and ligaments, but he explained to her that he was a Doctor of Physics, not a physician. He evaluated medical appliances and made recommendations to various doctors along the eastern seaboard. He thanked her for the opportunity to review Eastern Precision's line of products.

"Enough about me," he said. "Tell me about you."

She seemed a bit flustered. "Me. Oh. I am the office manager. I've been with the company for about three years. I started out as a packer, then moved on to a clerical assistant, then when Mrs. Clark left the firm, I was promoted to office manager. Mr. Sullivan is a great boss. And I'm very happy there."

"Sounds like you're a go-getter."

She blushed. "I'm just lucky. Life is like a cup of tea. It's all in how you make it." She laughed.

He smiled at her. "You haven't touched your drink, Margaret."

"Sorry, I'm so thrilled to be here. My mind drifted." She lifted her glass, looked him in the eye, and offered a toast. "*Fad saol agat.*"

"And a long life to you also."

He sipped, but she drank lustily. In seconds, any tenseness in her face drained away. Her eyes remained bright, but her gaze lingered. Currant marveled at the transition. "You look like you're enjoying yourself."

"That I am, Arthur." She nodded and offered a coy smile.

"Do you live nearby?

"I'm in St. Mary's parish. I've got a nice little apartment in a three-flat building just south of the plant. I can walk to work. Walk to church."

"Family?"

She hesitated before answering. Currant saw a tiny flash of pain on her face. "I do. I have a daughter, Mary. She's married now. Her husband's a fine man. And I have two sons. Mike is the youngest. He's eighteen. He's working at a C.C.C. camp near Syracuse. A place called Green Lakes State Park. They've got him working hard. But he's a good boy. He gets to keep five dollars a month. He sends me the rest. Twenty-five dollars. I'm keeping it in a bank for him."

"And your other boy?"

"That would be Patrick. He left home a couple of years ago. He couldn't find a job. And he just couldn't stand being at home with nothing to do."

"Jobs are hard to come by today," said Currant.

She sipped her drink. "Very…"

"Where does he live?"

She shook her head. "I don't know. He's on the road. Riding the rails. Once in a while, I get a card from him. The last one was from Seattle. He's quite the traveler."

"A young man seeking his fortune. I admire him."

"I guess…" she said. "But I miss him. I worry that things will get too bad."

"Well, you are a mother, Margaret."

She rolled her misty eyes and nodded.

"What about you, Arthur. Do you have a family?"

He pursed his lips. "Not anymore. My wife died quite a while back. We didn't have any children."

She looked at him with concern. "I'm so sorry."

"Thanks. And you are without a mate also…."

She dropped her head. "For about four years. I don't think I'll ever get over it."

"I understand. Was it sudden? Did he suffer?" Currant found himself questioning his words. They sounded clumsy and wooden.

She looked up at the ceiling.

"Sorry." He backtracked. "You see, my wife was ill for many years. I had plenty of time to adjust to living without her."

She thought for a moment. "I don't know...about the suffering." Her words came slowly. She swallowed hard. "One day, I went for a walk, and when I came home, I found him hanging from a rope on the back porch." She stared into space and spoke quietly without emotion. "He just left me with no goodbye and no good reason. I guess he couldn't handle the pain of being jobless and unable to support us. He did odd jobs and made a little money, but he was out of work for well over a year. I think he felt useless. I encouraged him to be hopeful. But the whole world had gone crazy. He became a shell of a man. Stayed inside himself. Drank more than he should have. But he didn't cause the problem. He was a hard worker and a good man. It was such a loss to the children and me."

At this strained moment in their conversation, the waiter appeared to take their orders. Currant was relieved. He had great sympathy for the woman and did not enjoy deceiving her. After that, over dinner, their talk turned to other more pleasant topics. At this point, they were both into their second round of drinks, and the conversation flowed easily. They seemed to have a natural affinity for each other. Quite smoothly, Currant dovetailed his interest in the health of President Roosevelt into the discussion. Margaret excitedly told him about the new leg braces that her company had fabricated. He pretended to be surprised by this revelation and asked her if he could see the braces on his upcoming factory tour. He was lucky, she said. They were to be shipped out tomorrow afternoon by Railway Express. After dinner, they made their way back to the hotel entrance. He insisted on taking her home. It was late, and Currant said he couldn't allow her to travel on public transportation alone. Also, he wanted to take the trolley across the East River; it would be his first trolley ride.

A short cab trip brought them to the station. Currant was visibly excited as the trolley rattled across the bridge headed for Queens. He sat on a bench next to Margaret, and they shared a perfect view of 1934 Manhattan at night. The trolley swayed, and Currant grabbed her hand.

She didn't resist. She looked at him and smiled.

"You're just a big kid, Arthur. Aren't you?"

"Why not?" he said. "I'm feeling young again."

The following day Currant arrived at the Eastern Precision Metal Fabrications building. Margaret greeted him. As he anticipated, she was all business. Last night as they stood on the front stoop of her apartment building, she had asked him not to reveal the fact of their dinner date to any of her coworkers. He agreed, but he demanded a kiss in ransom. She delivered.

Now, amidst her tough stand to convey an image of official behavior, he broke the spell by putting two fingers on his lips and silently blowing a kiss in her direction. She scoffed and used the intercom to summon Mr. Sullivan. He arrived in seconds, entered the lobby, and welcomed Currant. After Currant thanked Mrs. Dougherty for her help, the two men, moved through the reception area into the fabrication plant. Currant had properly primed his targets. Sullivan treated him as if he were royalty and showed the many types of orthopedic appliances in fabrication. Currant told him that leg braces were one of his particular interests.

"As a physicist, leg braces are fascinating devices. They are subject to extreme stress in lateral-torsional bending."

Sullivan smiled. "I can see that you are well aware of the demanding issues related to fabricating our braces. Mrs. Dougherty told me about your keen interest in our most famous client. Would you like to see them?"

Currant smiled. "Absolutely."

Sullivan escorted Currant by the arm to an area of the plant surrounded by heavy canvas curtains. He held back the curtain to permit Currant to pass. "Enter, my friend. You are in for a treat."

On the table, supported by work stands, two orthopedic soldiers stood proudly; with glistening metal and strapping black leather, they awaited the legs of the President to call them to duty. Currant took a deep breath. The possible means of FDR's demise lay before him. Fresh and clean, the metal was brightly polished, and the leather straps and bands appeared as fashionable as a new pair of men's wingtips. He eyed them carefully, knowing that any flaw in the construction of the joint or its locking mechanisms could bring down the most powerful man in America.

"So, Doctor," said Sullivan. "These are the new leg braces for the President. You will note they are constructed of aluminum which provides superior strength in a lightweight design. The joints of the double upright bars are reinforced with bronze bushings and steel rivets. For simplicity, we have provided aluminum ring drop locks at the knees. And compression spring drop foot braces with stirrup shoe attachments."

"Very impressive, Mr. Sullivan. May I inspect them closely?"

"Certainly, Doctor Gabriel."

A.C. Currant approached the work table and lifted a brace. Holding it above the table without strain, he thought it would not be a burden to wear, but then he remembered that FDR was required to wear braces on both legs every waking minute of his day, artificial constructs which supported his entire world. Currant examined the braces in detail, looking for potential faults in the knee locking mechanism and joint area. The newsreel movie had shown FDR's right knee caving in from the side. He found no indication of a defect in the metal work—no cuts, welds, abrasions, or hairline joints. Unseen by Sullivan, he tapped the metal lightly with his signet ring. He detected no hollowness or inconsistency and verified the leather straps, which were solid and effective. He studied the other leg brace. It also checked out. If the devices were to fail, there would have to be a weakness in the metal. He locked the knee joints and attempted to flex them. They were solid.

"You'll never be able to bend those joints, Doctor. These things are made to outlive the patient. The finest leg braces ever made. A hundred years from now, they'll be on display in some museum."

Currant replaced the brace on the work stand. "Very nice work. I'm sure the President will find them very satisfactory."

"He'll be moving from steel braces to aluminum. I suspect he will enjoy the weight difference and the ease and comfort of these."

"Thank you for the opportunity to inspect this bit of history," said Currant. "They look ready to go."

"We're on a deadline. Going out today." He turned away and yelled across the shop to a worker. "Al. Pack 'em up now." As they continued to talk, the man moved quickly into position in front of them. Currant observed him package the braces for transit. Sullivan continued his sales pitch to his new angel, Dr. Gabriel. "Hopefully, the President can test them out this weekend and use them for the opening day ceremonies at the ballpark next week. By the way, please mention our name to Senator Ferguson."

"I'll be delighted to do that, Mr. Sullivan." Currant checked his wristwatch and thanked the man for the tour. "It has been most enlightening. No need to show me out. I'll find the way." They shook hands, and Currant walked quickly to the office door. Margaret was standing at a file cabinet organizing its contents. She smiled when she saw him.

"Hope you enjoyed your tour, Doctor Gabriel."

"That I did, Mrs. Dougherty." He brushed past her on his way out, letting his hand briefly touch her thigh. "I hope we see each other again."

"Me too," she said, looking over her shoulder.

From the lobby area, he saw her once again. Silently she mouthed the words, "Thank you, Arthur."

He waved gently, opened the door into the sunlight, and began his journey back to Washington, D.C., confident that at this moment, FDR had nothing to fear, not even fear itself, because the braces were soundly constructed. Of course, he thought, someone could modify them in transit or upon arrival at the White House.

The odds were against these possibilities, but they remained in play.

-Chapter XII-

The Perfect Crime

"Did you have a good time?" asked Ethan.

"All business, boys. All business," said A.C. Currant.

"Right. How was your date?"

"She was very sweet. So, sweet that the next time I return, I'll be sure to see her again."

"High praise from you."

Currant smiled. "I'm not too old to appreciate a good woman when I see one. And she was accommodating in my leg brace investigation."

"So, you've said. To sum it up. Aluminum braces. State of the art. No funny business. Quality product," said Zak.

"What's next?" asked Ethan. "Today's Saturday. The baseball game is Tuesday. Are the new braces going to arrive in time for the game?"

Currant nodded. "That's for sure. Railway Express is delivering them. They're probably in the White House now."

"Should we walk over there?" asked Ethan.

"To the White House?"

"Right."

Currant laughed. "What could we do? Do you think anyone will invite us to check out FDR's new leg braces?"

"You're right. But the waiting's killing me," said Ethan.

"Just so it's not killing FDR," said Zak.

Ethan looked at this friend. "I think I preferred you as a mute."

"*Te Crees Muy,*" replied Zak.

Ethan shook his head. "You know, you toss out that lingo like you know what you're saying. But I know a little Spanish. And it makes no sense."

"It's slang. I'm into my south-of-the-border utterances.

"You want to enlighten us?"

"*Ciertamente no*! What fun would that be? You need to

lighten up, Ethan. We're in the 'killing time' phase of time travel. There's not much we can do. We should be having fun and enjoying ourselves. Yesterday, we met those two girls at the movie theater, and you treated them like they were diseased. We could be on a date tonight. Now you're complaining we've got nothing to do. Tell him, A.C., we're becalmed, right?"

Currant shrugged. "He's got a point. We can't do much. We could go to the White House and stare through the fence, watching for the Railway Express truck. But..."

Ethan checked his watch. It was 10:22 in the morning. "Fine. I think I'll just do that. I'm interested in solving problems, not screwing around."

"Hold your horses," said Currant. "Let me call Jack. I've got an idea. Maybe he can get a report from the White House. At least we'll know if they were delivered."

"Good," said Ethan. "Let's do it."

Currant placed the call. Ethan could hear that Jack answered. They spoke for just a few seconds, and Currant hung up. "I got the impression he doesn't want to talk on the hotel phone system. Too many ears for this topic. He's right. Any mention of the President may set off alarm bells for some nosy operator. I told him I'd get back to him in fifteen minutes. We need to find a payphone."

They rushed around the hotel room as if something was happening. For Ethan, any action was better than none. At least today was Saturday. They wouldn't have to don their suits and fedoras. They all shot out of the room and took the elevator to the main lobby of the Mayflower. A row of payphone booths awaited them. Ethan took the lead this time. "A.C., got a nickel?"

Currant frowned at him. "Did you go through all that cash I gave you?"

"No, mother. I'm out of change. And I want to make a call."

Currant rolled his eyes. "Here," he said as he handed him the coin. "Don't spend it all in one place."

Ethan took the nickel, entered an empty phone booth, sat down, closed the door, and pulled out a slip of paper bearing Jack's number. It was a quiet coffin except for the sound of a small fan tucked into the corner of the ceiling. He realized he wasn't sure what to do next. He read the directions above the phone dialer. Then he heard someone tapping on the door. He glanced up to see A.C. Currant staring at him.

"You need help?" Currant's muffled voice chided him. He and Zak were smiling.

"I got it. Don't worry." Ethan pulled the earpiece off the hook and held it while depositing the coin. A bell inside signaled as it slipped through the slot and dropped into the coin box with a clunk. He dialed Jack's number, who answered on the second ring.

"Jack. Ethan. I'm on a payphone in the hotel lobby."

"Good. What's up?"

"A.C. went to New York to track the items. They should have arrived in Washington by now. They're in A-1 condition, according to him. Or at least they were before they left."

"Well, we know that can't be. They're going to fail for some reason."

"Right. We need an update. We need to know where they are and their condition. We need to know who has access. Can you get it?"

Jack paused. "You know...it's not like I've got a direct line to the White House. Maybe I can get in touch with Mrs. R., and maybe she'll get back to me."

"I get that. The good news is that we have a few days. And you already told her that the Big Guy should not use the new items at the game. Right?"

"I made that point. But, obviously, we know who will make the final decision."

"You've got to try. There's nothing we can do."

"I'll put in the call as soon as we hang up. But it may take a while. If I can't get a hold of you, I'll leave a message with the hotel operator. OK?"

"Right. We'll wait," replied Ethan. "What else can we do?"

"Nothing."

Ethan paused to scratch the back of his head. "Jack. I forgot to mention something."

"What?"

"I think I saw your cowboy friend at the train station when Mr. Big returned from his fishing trip."

"You saw him. Did he see you?"

"I was a face in the crowd. I don't think so."

"Tall fellow with a tan hat?"

"Yep. Almost as tall as me."

"That's him. Keep an eye out for him. But don't attract attention. He's here to make sure that Mr. Big takes a dive."

"Got it. I'll tell Zak and A.C., and we'll keep a low profile."

"Good."

"Say hello to Emma for me."

Jack laughed. "I'll give her a kiss...from you." He hung up.

Ethan replaced the earpiece and squeezed out of the booth. He put off answering any questions until they were outside as a trio walking down Connecticut Avenue toward the White House. They spent the day taking turns watching all the entrances to the most famous building in Washington. At the end of the day, they had nothing. There was no sign of the cowboy man. A Railway Express truck did arrive late morning. But whether that truck delivered the leg braces remained unknown.

Over the next three days, they heard nothing from Jack. Tomorrow April 24, 1934, would be Opening Day. Back in the hotel room, the three time travelers anxiously waited. Zak seemed more excited about seeing his first major league baseball game than trying to stop FDR's political assassination.

"Zak, please stop talking about the stupid baseball game. We're running out of time."

Zak set down the newspaper's sports section for a moment, made a face, and then returned to his passion. Ethan looked over to A.C. Currant, who was listening to the radio while thumbing through a *Radio Guide* magazine that featured a portrait of FDR talking into a microphone on its cover. The magazine title proclaimed: *Franklin D. Roosevelt, President of the United States, His Most Powerful Weapon is the Radio.* Earlier, Ethan had read the article. In a way, it was surprising. Roosevelt did not hesitate to use the latest technology available to him. Anytime he wanted to speak directly to one-hundred-twenty-million Americans, he could get radio time.

Because of the novelty of radio as entertainment, people were always listening to it. When Roosevelt spoke, all other voices on the radio would be silenced. He could be heard live on every station. In the first three months of 1934, he had taken advantage of this propaganda superpower twenty-seven times, using his 'perfect radio voice' to sell his programs, quash any negative rumors, and bash antagonists. It was a bully pulpit that his fifth cousin and his wife Eleanor's uncle, President Teddy Roosevelt, would have relished. It was the first real-time, simultaneous direct connection to all the voters and every chief executive's dream. Unfortunately, the kind of political assassination planned for tomorrow afternoon could not be massaged away by a smooth-talking president. His fall and inability to rise, the aftermath with bloodied head, dirt, dishevelment, humiliation, and severe physical weakness exposed, would be viewed by millions at their local movie theaters over the next few weeks, assuring his demise. He would be unable to talk his way out of this one.

Currant sipped his Scotch while listening to 'The Goldbergs' radio show, a popular slice-of-life show featuring Gertrude Berg. He seemed engrossed. All very cozy thought, Ethan, but we're not the perfect family of 1934 listening to the radio, sipping an after-hours cocktail, and speculating about tomorrow's big game. The President of the United States, situated a few blocks away in the White House, having had his evening swim and finishing dinner with his wife and guests, was no doubt relaxing after a hard day's work. Ethan envisioned him holding court, wearing his Pince-Nez glasses, a martini in one hand and a cigarette holder in the other.

"Hey. Wake up, guys! We're out of time. I'm going to call Jack now." A.C. turned down the radio, and Zak looked over the top of his newspaper while Ethan grabbed his jacket and left the room hurriedly, leaving his companions to their diversions.

He dialed the phone and reached Jack on the first ring. "Jack, what the heck is going on?"

"Sorry, Ethan. Believe it or not. I just got off the phone with Irvin."

"Who's Irvin?"

"He's the Big Guy's valet."

"OK"

"Here's the story. The devices arrived on Saturday, and the Big Guy started using them the next day. Apparently, he likes them. Lightweight and very comfortable. He used them all day Sunday and today without any problem. According to Irwin, he's going to use them tomorrow."

"What?" asked Ethan. "I thought Mrs. R. agreed they would never be used for the game."

"She did, but she doesn't have the final say."

"So, what? There's nothing we can do? Did you ask the valet if he inspected them carefully?"

"Yes. First, he inspected the box when it arrived. There was no evidence that anyone tampered with it. And it was sealed with steel bands. He told me the receiving clerk had a tough time even opening the carton."

"Sounds good."

"A little later, they were brought to the Big Guy's bedroom. Irvin said he had spent a half-hour that morning examining them. He sounds like a sharp guy. And very cautious. He looked for any imperfection, cut, abrasion, or seam. He inspected them inch by inch. Of course, he couldn't see the areas under the leather strap wraparounds or the caution labels on the drop ring locks, but he could see that those areas all appeared untampered. He flexed each of them both for strength. There's no weakness. Anyway, they seem to work very well. He'll be wearing them tomorrow. I don't know, Ethan. I think we've done what we can do. I can't bother Mrs. R. anymore. She's already upset with me."

"She'll be more upset tomorrow if this whole thing goes bad."

"I hear you. Listen, I don't trust this cowboy guy. You've got tickets for the game, right?"

"Yep."

"Well, keep your eyes open. Supposedly, he's there to make sure things go as planned. But, he may be more than just an observer. We don't know how they will do it, but I feel this isn't being planned by any adversaries from this time. It's too difficult to execute. The devices are simple, strong, and foolproof. Everyone, including Currant, has taken a good look at them. And they've been tested by the man himself over the last two days. They work fine. So, it must be something else. A trip wire. A push. A shove."

"I saw the newsreel, Jack. There's no one near him. It's just him, the railing, and the ball. He tosses it and then goes down as if he was shot dead. He doesn't slip. He doesn't trip."

"Ethan. Hear me. You guys have done your best. There's nothing else to do. Go there. Eyes open. But don't call attention to yourselves. Or you may end up in jail. And you might just drag us into it. You're working without a net. Do you understand?"

Ethan thought. "We've come a long way just to watch, Jack."

Jack paused. "Sometimes, that's all you can do. We're not miracle workers, Ethan. Things happen."

"We'll see. If we can, we'll stop it. You'll know by tomorrow evening. Goodnight, Jack. Wish us luck."

"Good luck."

Ethan returned to the hotel room. He was despondent. He sat down and asked Currant if he might have a drink. Currant was surprised, as Ethan was not a very stable drinker.

"You must have bad news," said Currant as he handed him two fingers of Scotch. He poured two more glasses, one for himself and one for Zak. "Go ahead. Fire away."

Ethan related his phone conversation with Jack. It didn't take long, leaving them with little to discuss.

"So, we just watch for a tall man in a cowboy hat," said Currant.

"That's about it," replied Ethan.

Currant rubbed his chin. "Tell me about the valet. What exactly did he say about the new braces? Did he examine them in detail?"

"Jack said he did. He checked all the surfaces except those hidden by the leather straps and the caution labels wrapped around the ring stops and flexed them...."

"Wait a New York minute," said Currant smiling. "What cautionary labels? There were no labels on the leg braces I inspected."

"Maybe they put them on before they shipped them," suggested Zak.

Currant jumped out of his chair. "Hell no. I watched them being packed. The box was sealed shut. No labels on any part of them."

Sensing Currant's excitement, Ethan got more interested.

"Then those labels must have been applied afterward," said Zak.

"Not in transit," said Ethan. "I doubt that. The box was sealed with steel banding."

"Maybe they were loose in the box, and the receiving clerk just applied them when he saw them," offered Zak.

"Maybe, but Irvin, the valet, made no mention of that. I suppose it's possible," said Ethan. "But what's the big deal. Just small labels. Something like, 'Push Down Firmly to Lock' or something like that."

"Exactly," said A.C. Currant. "Ingenious. The labels. That's the answer. They may also say 'DO NOT REMOVE THIS LABEL'"

Ethan and Zak shrugged their shoulders.

"Don't you see? The labels are placed exactly at the

weak link. No doubt they're on the locking rings. Sure, the rings must be slid into place to keep the knee joint from flexing. It's a simple operation. And fool-proof. Once those rings are in place, the strut is rigid. Inflexible. Effective. The knee joint can't flex, and it can't bend."

"That's good, right? Am I missing something?" said Zak.

Currant smiled. "Do you know anything about the softening temperature of aluminum?"

"I think we missed that class," said Zak.

"Aluminum is lightweight. About one-third the weight of steel. Properly alloyed and heat-treated, it's solid. But it will start to elongate and weaken at high temperatures. Say a couple of hundred degrees Celsius."

"How's that going to happen?" asked Zak.

Currant nodded. "It's only a guess. But I think we're dealing with nano-thermite here. If those labels are nano-thermite impregnated, it would only take an igniter to activate them. I would guess just enough of the substance would instantly raise the temperature above the locking ring softening point. Then, any torsion in the strut would cause the ring to fail and the knee joint to lose its rigidity."

"Torsion...like tossing out the first pitch?" asked Ethan.

"Exactly," said Currant."

"It would have to be perfectly timed."

"Yes. The heat reaction would happen instantaneously. Someone would have to wait, watch and then cause the ignition."

"How?" asked Zak.

"This is not 1934 technology, my friends. This must have been planned by someone from our time. But, to answer your question. I would guess they would use an RF module."

Zak nodded. "When I was young, I used those to control my model airplanes."

Currant continued. "A radio frequency device. The push of a button would activate a chip, ignite the nano-thermite, and cause the locking rings to fail. You wouldn't even have to have line-of-sight except for the timing. You'd have to be watching the President's arm. Just when he began to bring his arm forward, they would push the button. With his foot locked firmly into position, the leg would flex from the throwing movement. But at this point, his knee joint would be like jelly. And down he would go."

"Wow. I think you have it, A.C.," said Ethan. "You're a genius."

Currant reached for his glass and downed the remainder of the drink. "That I am, boys. That I am." He sat down on the sofa, looking very pleased with himself.

Zak seemed puzzled. "But wouldn't the high temperatures burn the President's legs?"

"For sure," said Currant. "If he could feel it, I would guess the pain would be intense."

"There was a strange look on FDR's face when he fell," said Ethan. "Weird. Surprised, or in pain, or both."

"With the onset of such pain, he would release his grip on the railing. He would lose all control."

"But everyone would know," said Zak. "They would know his braces were the cause of the fall."

Currant chuckled. "How the hell would anyone from 1934 explain what happened. Most likely, the aluminum ring locks would be deformed or even snapped as if they failed. If the amount of nano-thermite was carefully calculated, only the skin on his legs near the ring locks would be burned. The entire phony label and its micro-solid-state circuitry would self-destruct, leaving only traces behind. It's a perfect crime."

"And the person who pushes the button?"

Currant shook his shoulders. "He's a guy with his hand in his jacket pocket in the upper row of the lower deck so far away from the action that he would appear uninvolved. Remember, he only has to push a button and then match his emotions to the other people in the stands. He'll appear surprised, shocked, amazed, and saddened by the event. Then he'll head back to the future."

-Chapter XIII-

The First Pitch

The three time travelers walked from the Mayflower Hotel to the ballpark. The walk reminded them they were living in the Great Depression. Almost every street corner had well-dressed men selling apples for a nickel a piece. Other jobless men wandered about wearing sandwich-board advertising placards hung from their shoulders. Soup kitchens for the hungry weren't visible, but the time travelers were well aware of them. Washington was a government town, so the drifters and homeless were less evident than in other big cities, but as they neared the ballpark, the foot traffic increased along with the number of panhandlers. Ethan was particularly affected by the young children who roamed the streets wildly in small packs, begging and pleading for a few coins. Each one had a sad story, well-rehearsed and designed to tug the baseball fans' hearts. Ethan and Zak depleted their nickels and dimes and bought a few smiles from the kids before arriving at Griffith Stadium,

They had tickets in hand. Even though the game wouldn't start for another hour and a half, a large portion of the twenty-five thousand people who would watch the game had already arrived. It was Ethan and Zak's first baseball game. Currant, who was almost a man of these times, had seen many games. He even claimed to have been to a World Series game held in Boston in 1986. Ethan and Zak weren't sure whether this was fact or fiction. The aging physicist often told stories that he remembered as reality but might only be the commingled memories of a man who had accumulated eight decades of life on the planet.

Today, the Washington Senators would play the Boston Red Sox in the annual home opener. It was a warm day, and unlike the rainout of the previous week, the sky was clear and bright. As they approached the Florida Avenue entrance of the massive stadium building, even Ethan had to admit that the anticipation of the game was contagious. The shouts of vendors hawking programs and other baseball memorabilia mixed with the rising garbled babble of thousands of people gyrating like bees in a hive. Pungent odors of steamed hot dogs and salted popcorn oozed out of the building tantalizing his taste buds. They walked up the long ramp leading to the entrance of the cathedral of baseball, and at the top, they passed through the ratcheting turnstiles, sliding out of the hot sun into the cool darkness of the confines.

At that moment, they became baseball fans. Crowd noise increased. They shuffled up the ramp to the lower deck as part of a mass of others. Shoulder to shoulder with hundreds of fans, they began the annual pilgrimage into the baseball shrine. Except for the children, the fans dressed for the occasion with most men, including the time travelers, wearing suits or sports coats with hats and ties. Women were also in the crowd, although in smaller numbers, dressed in what seemed to Ethan elegant outfits. Opening day was a boisterous mixture of fun and pomp, with the players and the audience dressed for their parts. As they drifted toward the sacred field of dreams, the pilgrims gathered strength at refreshment stands and purchased scorecards and other relics to remember the event.

When the ramp leveled out, Ethan glanced to his left. The view of the field was spectacular. In the cool darkness, the regimented stadium seating sloped down, boldly opening onto a vast plateau of green and brown bathed in blazing sunlight. The contrast was striking. Ethan tapped Zak on the shoulder and pointed to the playing field. They both stopped in their tracks but soon were prodded on by a smiling Currant.

"Pretty impressive, isn't it?" shouted Currant.

Zak and Ethan could only nod their heads in appreciation of the sight.

In time, they reached Section D and found their seats

in the lower deck's upper crannies. They had a clear view of the spectators and the ball field from the top row of seats. These were not the best seats to watch the game, but they offered a decent view of Franklin Roosevelt's luxury box just above the first base side dugout.

Ethan gazed out at the field. There was a sloping ramp leading to the Presidential box. He assumed that FDR would enter this way. Beyond that, the players were warming up, practicing throwing, catching, and pitching. The seats in the grandstands were now about half-filled. Flags and bunting celebrating opening day hung from the stadium's upper deck. Ethan was surprised to see the irregularity of the playing field. The entire structure backed up to a residential neighborhood. The outfield was roughly rectangular, with the left-field home-run wall a greater distance than the right-field wall. There were no seats in right field, and its enclosing wall and the integrated scoreboard formed a high wall. He guessed it was taller to equalize the distance for a home run. Most strangely, the center-field perimeter notched around the backyards of some houses adjacent to the stadium; the tops of trees beyond the wall seemed incongruous.

"Ethan. It's time to go to work," said Currant. "We have to find our man. I would guess that no matter how powerful his RF module is, he will take no chances. He has only one shot at it. He'll be relatively near. Close enough to see all the President's movements. You agree?"

Ethan nodded. "I only saw him once at the train station. He's very tall and, according to Jack, never without his cowboy hat. We can hope," said Ethan.

"You want us to take the flanks?" asked Zak.

"Yes. I'll stay here. You guys should take positions along this back wall. You'll have a view of everyone below," said Currant. "If you see him. You have to approach him and stop him from using the transmitter. If you can, make it look like an accident. But you'll only have one chance. So, don't blow it."

The game would start shortly. Excited baseball fans munching, smoking, and drinking filled the seats. Ethan and Zak got up and took positions on the walk behind. They paced back and forth, Zak on the right and Ethan on the left. They looked for the man in the cowboy hat while Currant remained seated, scanning the area. Ethan heard someone walking above him and glanced up. Several uniformed policemen stood watch, and half-dozen other men dressed in civilian clothes also patrolled the catwalk. One of the cops looked down, and Ethan quickly turned his attention to the scene below. Clearly, the group on the catwalk was a security detail who could easily monitor the location from their vantage point.

Franklin Roosevelt's box stood out. Layers of bunting covered the low wall above the dugout area. Distinguished dignitaries, some in naval uniforms, sat in the special box. Just then, the crowd began to stir. Something was happening. A phalanx of Washington Senator ballplayers stood along the first base line while the Boston Red Sox players formed a line on the third-base side. Ethan spotted an open-top automobile slowly moving along the right field baseline. Security agents rode the running boards and walked adjacent to the car's four corners. The crowd cheered. Soon Franklin Roosevelt's familiar visage came into view. Wearing a broad smile, he waved to the masses.

The car slowly pulled up in front of the dugout and then stopped. It was difficult for Ethan to see the President exiting the vehicle from his location. All the fans in the stands were on their feet. A crowd of security men surrounded the side of the car. Briefly, he saw FDR holding a cane in his hand and aided by a man at his side, walking in his peculiar manner toward the sloping ramp leading into the stands. He disappeared into the crowd as it was announced that the President of the United States had arrived. "Hail to the Chief" played, and the crowd cheered. FDR raised his hand and waved. Ethan now knew where the President stood. News photographers and motion picture cameras were set up on the field about twenty feet below FDR's seat.

Ethan knew a tall man like the cowboy would have the

viewing advantage. But Ethan was quite tall, and even he found it challenging to follow the President's movements. The crime would have to be executed with perfect timing. The remote-control electronic signal would have to be transmitted to the nano-thermite chips just as the President's arm began its forward-throwing movement. Moe Berg, the Senators' catcher, stood on the turf below the Presidential box, waiting for the ball. The crowd's enthusiasm made the view toward FDR more tenuous. Occasionally, someone would stand on a seat, attempting to get a better look. Seconds later, the violator would be talked back into his seat by the people behind whose views were blocked. Everyone was contending to see the President.

The players along the baselines stood at attention, facing center field. An American flag waved in the distance. Then, from loudspeakers, the 'Star-Spangled Banner' played. Everyone, including Ethan, froze in place. Ethan pretended to be singing, but he didn't know the lyrics. As he mouthed silent words, he scanned the crowd looking for tall men. In 1934, men taller than six feet were not the norm.

Some looked like possibilities. One of them was working a hot dog cart. Tall and similar in build to the cowboy man, he wore a white vendor cap. He wasn't singing the anthem; he was focused on the area of the Roosevelt box. A young customer, a boy waving a dollar bill, approached him. He waved the kid away. It seemed odd.

Another possible assassin stood at the front railing about a hundred feet to the left of FDR, too far to be an obvious threat but still within range of a modern RF module. He, too, was intently staring in the direction of FDR's seating area. But everyone was looking toward the Presidential box. They all knew Roosevelt would soon be opening the game.

Halfway through the anthem, something was happening in the area of the hot dog man. Reacting to the disturbance, there was a rumble from the crowd. A heavy man wearing a straw hat held a boy in one arm and argued with the vendor. The vendor tried to ignore him. Ethan signaled Zak to go there. Soon several uniformed men appeared on the scene and surrounded the vendor, the kid, and the angry man.

Ethan took one more look back at Zak. His friend was standing near the cops, the vendor, and the disgruntled customers. The cops had grabbed the vendor and were taking him away. Zak flashed Ethan a 'thumbs up,' but Ethan suspected the event could be a diversion.

Searching the people behind him, he saw one man in a sea of faces who ignored the hot dog disturbance. The suspect, who remained focused on the boxes eighty feet below, stood near an opening in the rear wall of the stadium, but the glare of the sunlight entering the darkened area made it difficult to see him. The anthem singing ended, and Ethan sensed FDR would soon stand to throw out the first pitch.

The target behind wore a blue baseball cap with a "C" above the bill. No cowboy hat, but Ethan was confident this was the man. He called out to Currant and Zak, but the crowd noise was too loud. He glanced up at the man again. Something metallic reflected in the sunlight, and Ethan recognized it as a polished chrome Zippo lighter. It was a perfectly innocuous device and one that would arouse no suspicion in anyone's mind. But for Ethan, it was a giant red flag. It could be the trigger device.

He politely fought off the fans in the aisle struggling to get a better view of FDR. It would have been easy for the physically dominating Ethan to push and shove people out of his way, but he didn't want to become the center of attention. Not long ago, he and the time-cop stared at each other for a brief moment at Union Station. Maybe the cowboy would recognize him. The public-address announcer spoke again. His voice echoed through the stands. *"Ladies and gentlemen, in a few moments, the first pitch will be thrown by the President of the United States, Franklin Delano Roosevelt."*

Sounds of anticipation and activity rose from below.

Ethan assumed FDR was moving into position to toss out
the ball. Making his way through the knot of fans, Ethan
stood just a few feet from his cowboy quarry. Impulsively
he decided to confront the man. He retrieved the prop
pack of Camel cigarettes from his front pocket, fumbled
with the cellophane and tin foil, struggling to open the
package, and tapped out a cigarette like Gary Cooper in
the movies. With unknown skill, he grabbed the cigarette
with his lips. Sunlight from the nearby window
momentarily blinded him; he couldn't see the man's face.
But he could see his hands. The man held his lighter
tightly in his left hand and an unlit cigarette in his other.
Ethan dug into his pants pocket as if searching for a pack
of matches. He pretended that someone had pushed him,
and he nudged the man and looked up at him.

"Got a light, Mac?" Ethan mumbled with the unlit
cigarette dangling. He didn't look at the man but faced
the ballfield.

"Not now," said the cowboy. "Out of fluid."

Ethan took a quick glance back. "Got a match?" The
time-cop put his unlit cigarette in his mouth, reached into
his pocket, and pulled out a pack of matches. Maintaining
his view of the scene below, he set his hand on Ethan's
shoulder.

"Keep it," he said with a degree of urgency and
annoyance.

Ethan looked back and grabbed the matches.
"Thanks." His mind flashed on the newsreel footage of
FDR throwing the ball and taking a terrible dive.

The stadium speakers came to life again. "*And now the
first pitch of the 1934 season will be delivered by our
President Franklin Roosevelt....*"

Ethan assumed the open lid of the lighter had armed
the RF module. The man held it in front of his face, but
he wasn't looking at it. His focus was on the action of the
President below. He waited. Anyone watching might think
he was transfixed by the ceremony and unwilling to miss
this historic moment in time. The time-cop, in the process
of lighting his cigarette, froze. He held the lighter in his

right hand and positioned the index finger of his left hand, ready to flip it shut. When that cover closed, the nano-thermite would ignite, and the rigid joints of FDR's braces would turn to jelly.

Ethan relived the newsreel of the first pitch. This was the moment. The crowd roared as FDR stood facing the field, wearing a dark double-breasted suit and his typical soft grey fedora. His body was immovably rigid and precariously balanced on his new aluminum leg braces. Ready to throw the pitch, he held the game ball in his right hand, smiled like a little boy, and grasped the metal rail in front. He tightened his grip on the railing, bracing himself for the coming movement of his very muscular upper body. Such an abnormal thrust always threatened to topple him. FDR knew how to counteract this threat but could never be prepared for his leg braces to collapse beneath him. He raised his arm, assuming a throwing position.

With his hands shaking, Ethan struck the match, held the flame under the cigarette, and took a deep drag. For the first time in his life, cigarette smoke entered his lungs. Nicotine struck home; it felt like someone had hit his chest with a baseball bat. He coughed violently, and in an almost seizure-like fit, he swung around and faced the time-cop. Another massive cough erupted, and his head and body drove forward into the assassin. Determined to stop the man from flipping the lighter lid to complete the circuit, Ethan's handmade hard contact with the cowboy knocking the lighter out of the man's hand. He looked up and saw the Zippo spin through the air, sunlight reflecting off its polished metal surfaces, finally disappearing out the window opening. Somewhere in the back of his mind, Ethan concocted the hopeful image of the lighter landing harmlessly on the pavement several stories below.

The crowd cheered wildly as FDR's toss found its mark safely in Moe Berg's catcher's mitt. The President waved to Berg and the raucous crowd, then returned to his seat.

The stadium announcer's voice boomed out. *"Play*

ball!"

"You idiot!" The cowboy shouted as he pushed Ethan away with great force.

Ethan pulled himself together and stood upright before the man. Bent over and between coughs, he spoke. "I'm sorry, buddy. Here, let me light your cigarette." He mumbled his words because his cigarette was still dangling from his lips, smoldering like a tiny white stick of dynamite.

The cowboy's face was flushed and red. "Stupid idiot!" He hyperventilated and clenched his fists as if he would pop Ethan in the jaw. Then he looked around almost in a daze, gathered his senses, and rushed down the aisle picking his way through the crowd and rapidly moving toward the exit.

Ethan dropped the Camel, crushed it with his foot, turned, and headed back to A.C. Currant. Zak arrived at the same time. Ethan beamed.

"Mission accomplished?" asked Currant.

Ethan, shaking with excitement, gave them the 'thumbs-up' signal. "I almost choked to death on my cigarette, but we did it. I believe our friend the cowboy believes he was the victim of bad luck."

"Yowsah. Yowsah. Yowsah," said Currant. "Every assassin should have a backup plan when the three of us are on duty."

Zak laughed. "*Echale ganas!*" he exclaimed. "I saw it all. You're the man, Ethan! Not much of a smoker, but one hell of a crime-fighter. Now, let's sit down and enjoy the game. Watch for good old number three, Heinie Manush; he's on an All-Star start this season."

As they sat next to each other with Currant in the middle, the old physicist threw his arms around his two time-traveling buddies. "Let's get some hot dogs and beer, fellows. We've got some celebrating to do."

LOG of Zak Newman
April 27, 1934 (local time): 14:32 (Day 18 of time travel)

We said our long goodbyes to Emma and Jack. Lots of tears and hugs and kisses. Tomorrow we will be heading back to the future. It's been a great and successful trip. We've managed to keep FDR at the helm. He's a happy man. He likes his leg braces.

Jack said a young man, a temporary worker in the White House receiving room, admitted to applying the labels. Tom Braedon, the cowboy time-cop bribed him to do the deed. Most likely, he was given a phony cover story by Braedon that someone at the factory forgot to install the warning labels, and that he could make a few extra dollars by making things right. The bad guys had a workable plan, but we busted the whole deal with a bit of luck and a ballsy attitude. Unfortunately, the Senators lost the game to Boston—5 to zip. Heinie Manush was 0 for 4. But still, you can't beat fun at the old ballpark.

Strangely, Jack had a meeting with Braedon the day after the unsuccessful political assassination attempt. They met, at the cowboy's request, in a parking lot in Rock Creek Park. Apparently, he's now a man on the run. Immediately after leaving the game, he attempted to contact his superiors to report his failure to complete his mission. But, he was unable to establish contact. There was no response to his message. He wanted to confirm that Jack was experiencing the same communication issues. Jack told him that his communicator was also not working.

Braedon feared for his life. He could never return to the future. He believed they would send a team to get rid of him. Knowing he was a marked man, he was going underground. The two of them made a pact. Braedon said that he had been sent to spy on Jack in addition to eliminating FDR. Their superiors suspected Jack might be a potential defector. But shortly after their first meeting, Braedon had reported there was no evidence that Jack might not return to the future. His deception was done in the interest of self-preservation. He wanted some insurance. He knew if he failed in the assassination attempt, he was toast. He needed someone to cover for him, and Jack was his man. Braedon suspected that Jack was committed to living in the past, but he had no interest in Jack's possible defection.

And he told Jack that in time, maybe in a few weeks, a body would float to the surface of the C & O canal. It would be that of a homeless drifter who matched Braedon's physical description. Presumably, Braedon had killed the man and had placed him in the dirty waters of the canal sometime before the opening day game. Braedon said their superiors might, at the very least, contact Jack about the whereabouts of the missing cowboy time-cop. In that case, Jack could feign ignorance but agree to do some digging and then present the cover story.

That was it. Braedon's final suggestion was that if Jack wanted to defect, he should move as far away from Washington as possible. His suggestion was Los Angeles. Everyone in the future would be moving to California. Jack had no idea where Braedon chose as his hideout. But he thought it would be somewhere that welcomed cowboys. My guess is Argentina.

End 04-27-34

-Chapter XIV-

Fishing for Traitors

The two time-traveling lovers, Emma and Jack, had settled into their new life as a couple in 1934. It was a cozy and intimate arrangement, given the size of Jack's apartment. Still, like many other young, unmarried, childless people in the time of the Great Depression, they were simply happy to be in love, employed, and able to enjoy life. Three months had passed since Ethan, Zak, and Doctor Currant had accomplished their mission and returned to Mystic Heights. While Emma carried an empty spot in her heart for her family and friends from her other life, she was also confident she had made the right decision. Jack continued his troubleshooting for Mrs. Roosevelt, and Emma had decided to become a freelance writer. The opportunity to make a decent living was slim, but she met new people, gained a better understanding of the times, and most importantly, enjoyed her work.

It didn't take long for Emma to establish credibility as a writer. Mrs. Roosevelt had penned a short letter of recommendation for her use, but it still rested in the desk drawer, unused. She had carved out her niche by continuing her work as an observer of the economic maelstrom. Her previous work as a writer for Mrs. Roosevelt had given her contacts and credibility with the local newspapers. She had her own byline now, using the pen name E.C. Wright, and she had gathered a small but faithful following of readers. Her human-interest stories described ordinary people's personal suffering, hardship, and bravery. In three months, she had several articles published in small local newspapers which exposed the personal stories of individuals caught in the crosswinds of the crisis.

Jack and Emma worked as a team. They believed their

efforts were contributing to a better world now and in the future. They retained their faith in FDR, as did the people of America. Each day the President grew stronger politically. While times remained tough, he was a confident and resolute leader. His army of conscripted Conservation Corps young men replanted the deforested and eroded lands, and his public works program, while inefficient, provided work in a land of unemployment. The Blue Eagle emblem of the NRA still flew high as a public relations tool, but its commander General Johnson, *Time* magazine's 'Man of the Year', appeared to be having trouble staying aloft. His rough personal approach and the inherent complications of the price-fixing program reduced his popularity. However, other New Deal programs kept up the people's hopes and gave them faith in the future. Most importantly, the country still had a democratically elected leader. Unlike the fascist or communist dictators of Europe, the traditional American government, albeit slightly modified, appeared to be working.

Thanks to the efforts of Emma and Ethan's commando group from the future, the planned opening day *coup* at the Washington Senator's Griffith Stadium had failed. And Jack continued to work to derail any efforts by the anti-Roosevelt forces to remove the President from office. He reported back to the future. He believed he had successfully maintained his time-cop role. However, Jack noticed that transmissions from the future were more sporadic and less clearly stated. He and Emma wondered if changes were rippling ahead in time because of their efforts to save FDR. It seemed as if something different was happening, although it was impossible to know. For the moment, it didn't matter. The time-cop, Tom Braedon, was no longer a threat, and the present was a good place to be. Jack focused on his next move with General Butler.

Emma took the lead. Jack gave her the phone number, and she contacted the General. He was about to cut her short until she mentioned her part in the 1932 Bonus Marcher movement. She told him about the Sweeny family and that she had narrowly escaped the fire and destruction when President Hoover's troops razed the encampment in Anacostia. He listened. She explained that she was writing an article about the veterans and their success or failure to get the Bonus money promised to them by Congress. She arranged to meet him at his home, a few miles outside Philadelphia. Jack and Emma agreed that she should go alone. The General might remember his previous meeting with Jack at the V.F.W. convention last year in Milwaukee. Questions would be asked. For their plan to work, there could be no connection between the Roosevelts and Butler. General Butler must never know that Jack was the one who arranged the initial meeting with the plotters, and he must not know that he worked for Eleanor Roosevelt.

Emma borrowed Jack's car that hot late July morning. She left Washington and drove east through Baltimore and Wilmington before turning north toward Newtown Square, Pennsylvania. She enjoyed the ride along the twisting country road. Compared to Jack's old Buick, the Airflow was fun to drive and luxurious. She missed the Buick's open-top, but she couldn't help but marvel at the rapid improvements in automobile design; the streamlined teardrop-shaped Chrysler Airflow replaced the boxy Buick. Its steel body, aluminum engine, and low profile set it apart from the competition. People gawked at her and the car, and she felt like Amelia Earhart without wings. Driving this car was the perfect expression of controlled power, independence, and freedom she had been unable to experience in her future life.

The time passed quickly. Soon Emma spotted General Butler's estate. The house was surrounded by old trees and set back from the road. She pulled into the drive and drove to the front of the large, boxy, two-story, stucco-clad house. Grabbing her leather-bound notebook, she exited her car. Except for the sound of birds chirping, the countryside location was tranquil. Her shoes crunched on the gravel leading to the portico. As she stepped onto the porch, a light gust of wind caught her hair, and she brushed it back with her hand. When she looked up, the entry door opened. Retired General Smedley Butler, ramrod fit and trim, his hawk-like face sculptured and leathery, looked precisely like the warrior she expected. She imagined him in Marine dress blues. Now sporting a summer suit and tie, he greeted her with a smile. As she approached him, he extended his hand to shake.

"Hello, Emma. I'm General Butler."

She looked down at the man. He was a few inches shorter than her, mid-fifties, with a shock of dark brown hair tinged with gray. His smile was sweet and genuine. Instantly, she liked him. Beneath all the fire and brimstone, the double Medal of Honor winner was a real man. "I hope you know how honored I am to meet you, sir." Her movement took on the elements of a bow, and she could tell he was both pleased and somewhat embarrassed by her show of deference.

"Come in." He escorted her along the long, two-story-high corridor, which was capped by a stair. Their footsteps clattered from the hardwood floor and echoed off the plastered walls. It was a cavernous hall that led to a large living room flooded with natural light from a wall of windows in a flanking, continuous enclosed porch. The room was a museum of artifacts, memorabilia, and trophies collected by Butler throughout his military career. Emma was awed by the display. The General simply smiled and directed her to sit on the sofa while he chose a wing chair. A heavy-set female servant entered and offered them drinks. Small talk between them filled the time for the woman to leave and return with two glasses of iced tea. She served them and then left the room.

They were alone. While the General waited patiently, Emma looked down as if to gather her thoughts. She focused on his glistening shoes and knife-edge creases in the cuffs of his pants. He was all military. She summoned her courage and moved ahead. "General Butler, I'm here for two reasons."

His eyebrows arched.

"First, I would like to know how you stand in your battle to secure the bonuses for the veterans. As I mentioned on the telephone, I was at Anacostia in the summer of '32. I was gassed and almost died in the fire. For a while, I lived with the veterans. I slept in the Sweeny family's cardboard and tarpaper shack. I was there. Like you, I have a commitment to the veterans and the country. And I want to report this story to the public accurately. It is important."

"And the second..." he asked. "You didn't mention another topic when you called."

She could tell the General was a soldier who sought a clear objective. He was not expecting another topic. "I did not. Would you prefer to take them in order?"

"If you were not such a pretty young gal, I might send you to the brig, but considering your beauty and me maintaining my reputation as a gentle warrior, why don't we tackle the real reason you're here. Let's call it, 'the real objective.'" He smiled, revealing an openness that was welcoming.

She nodded. "Thank you. I appreciate that. But I hope we will have time to gather all the facts on veterans."

"One target at a time...go on, Emma. Lead the charge."

"Unfortunately, this matter is the most important and most urgent."

"More important than my veterans getting what they deserve?"

She looked 'The Fighting Quaker' directly in his eyes. "That is a question for you to decide, sir." She gave him an edgy look.

He leaned in toward her. "If you don't mind me asking...how old are you?"

"Twenty-three."

"My daughter, Ethel, is a bit older than you. And I'll tell you what I told her when she was just a youngster. I started fighting with the Marines when I was sixteen. And I spent a lot of time shooting at ghosts in the boondocks. Every jungle monkey in a tree would get my attention. But I never hit a ghost or a monkey. If you have something in your sights...shoot. Now tell me exactly what's on your mind. Bottom line."

She cleared her throat. "I'm here to help stop a takeover of the government. A *coup d'état*. The removal of President Franklin Roosevelt from office."

He leaned back in his chair. "That's a mouthful. And I don't think it's just a latrine rumor. Let me guess. Does this have anything to do with those boys from that Sound Dollar Committee?"

"It does. Yes, sir."

"And how do you know about them?"

She inhaled deeply. "This is where I ask you to trust me. I can't exactly tell you."

The General's face morphed into stone. "That's not a good answer. Or at least it's not an answer which will continue our conversation." He waited.

She rolled her eyes. "I didn't think so. The fact is, I don't know that the *coup* will happen. But I know there have already been attempts to remove the President."

General Butler cocked his head. "Are you talking about that nutcase in Miami?"

She nodded. "That's one. That Italian guy who was electrocuted was not the assassin. His bullets found their target. Mayor Cermak. But someone else had been hired to shoot the President. A different plot. That attempt was stopped."

"And you know this how?"

"My fiancé was there. But this must never be revealed."

"I'm listening," he said. "Who's behind all this?"

She took a sip of her drink, mentally chose her words, and proceeded. "It's those same people who hired you to maintain the *status quo* in those little countries down south. The people who run the 'racket,' as you call it."

"And your source of information. Your fiancé. Why was he in the line of fire?"

"I can tell you he was hired to ensure that nothing happened to Mr. Roosevelt. But I would be putting him in danger to say anything more." She paused. "I can't give you his name. I guess at this point, I would have to say he is most important to me. Ahead of the veterans. Ahead of FDR."

Butler pursed his lips. "OK, I get it. Spill the rest. I'll listen. What's next? What about the Sound Dollar boys?"

"Have you spoken with them recently?"

"You're talking about that fellow MacGuire and his millionaire chum Robert Clark."

She nodded.

"The last time I saw either of them was last September. Oh. And I also got postcards from MacGuire from Europe every so often at the beginning of this year. Postcards. Like he's on vacation. Italy, Germany, France, Spain. But tell me, you're not suggesting these guys are anything to worry about? They couldn't find their...." He stopped himself. "Anyway, I wrote them off. Are they for real?"

Emma nodded. "I'm afraid they are. And right now, you are the only direct connection to the plot. These people want to use you. If they can. Have they promised you anything? Have they said they would help the veterans? Because that's what they want from you. They want the power you control over those hundreds of thousands of trained soldiers and use that to take over the government."

General Butler rose from his chair and began to pace back and forth. "I told them to buzz off. If they wanted my help, they never offered much in the way of *quid pro quo*. They made some references to getting the Bonus paid. They talked about taking over the American Legion. They wanted a gold-backed dollar. I got the point they didn't think much of FDR. But, these fellows are dingbats. One guy has a metal plate in his head from a war wound, and the other guy, Clark, served with me in China. He's a rich goof. A ne'er-do-well. Lots of money, but not much else. You can't be serious."

"I'm serious. Recently there was another attempt to take the President down by destroying his reputation. This attempt was also stopped. It's most likely the same people. The rich and the powerful. They don't like to have their power taken away."

He stopped pacing and stood before her. "What kind of attempt?"

"They rigged his leg braces so that he would fall on his face in public. We stopped that."

"Who's we?"

"My brother and his friends."

Butler scratched the top of this head as if digging a mental foxhole. "We'll you come to me with the most outlandish story, young lady. If I didn't already know the world was a crazy place, I wouldn't believe it. But it is, and I do."

"Fair enough, General. Our country needs your help again. We're a nation of laws...not guns. This is not a banana republic...yet."

"Not yet." He pursed his lips. "Not yet. OK, I hear you. As far as I can tell, these guys that you say are planning a *coup* are just fishing around. That's all. I listened to them. But their story is not as clear as you are. As a matter of fact, if I brought any of this to the surface, I would get laughed out of town. They wouldn't have to deny anything because they were just spouting off. Not the worst stuff I have heard about Mr. Roosevelt, I might add. Look, I'm no big fan of the President. We get no support from him. He put through that Economy Act, and shut down pensions and benefits to the veterans. If I had a blacklist, he'd be on it. But I am a red-blooded American. Maybe I was duped into being an enforcer for the banana republic boys, but I'm working on exposing that. You must have heard something since you mentioned my 'war is a racket' comments. Anyway, I would never be part of any effort to replace a duly elected public official."

"I know that, General. But you're the potential weak link in the bad guys' chain of events. We believe that their most recent failure to get rid of FDR the easy way will cause them to attempt the more difficult approach...the *coup*. We think General Johnson could be involved. Or maybe he is just being set up to take over. But in either case, he is in position for a possible transition. But, if you could string them along just enough for them to expose themselves, maybe they could be checkmated."

Butler sat down and rubbed his chin. "You know," he said quietly, "it's just not in my nature to play games like this. But I'm up for the challenge. Where do we go next?

"The next move is theirs. If they don't contact you again, that means they have gone in another direction. But based on what you have told me, they may. After all, potentially, you could command a half-million troops who could overwhelm the White House. And back up any scheme these plotters may have in mind. Of course, FDR has the military...."

"Which is a minimal force right now," interjected Butler.

"Yes. And he also has the Civilian Conservation Corps. A quarter-million or so untrained men. Many of whom might be looking for a new leader. Who knows? Like General Johnson."

"Well, I'll tell you right now. I'm never going to tell these plotters that I will help them take over the White House."

"No. I wouldn't think you would. But you could provide just enough rope to hang themselves. Let's see what develops. If they contact you again, just be a little more receptive. Throw out the bait, and let them hook themselves."

He laughed. "Fishing for traitors. OK, I'm in. If this thing looks like it's going to pop, I'll make sure it doesn't. I'll send them all home in wooden overcoats."

She laughed. "General, you're the best." The young woman and the old soldier talked for another fifteen minutes about the potential *coup*. Any new attempt by the bad guys to make contact with Butler would be a subject of notification to Emma. She gave him the phone number of a reporter friend at the *Washington Daily News* who could take a message. With that topic closed, Emma interviewed the General regarding the veterans' cause. He was more at ease in this conversation. He brought her up to date on the progress of his quest for the Bonus.

Franklin Roosevelt seemed to have little interest in

justice for the veterans. He was not actively working with Congress to pass a bill that would mandate an early payment of the veterans' Bonus money. As far as Butler was concerned, FDR was no better than Hoover except that Hoover had burned them out of Washington D.C. in 1932. Emma expressed sympathy for the Bonus Marcher's cause, and she had one suggestion for Butler's consideration. It was something that she and Jack had discussed. "General Butler. Have you ever thought that FDR might be inclined to pay your boys the Bonus, but he can't get the money?"

This statement seemed to light a fire under the General. His face turned red. "What? All the money that's wasted in Washington? Those bastards... sorry. Those politicians toss away more money in one day than I could earn in a lifetime. There's no excuse!"

Emma continued in the face of his anger. "It's the bankers, I believe. They control the money. They want to get their cut. And President Roosevelt has no shortage of programs to spend the available cash in the treasury. I have an idea for your consideration. You should suggest that the Bonus money should be in the form of bonds that can be turned in for cash immediately. This way, the bankers will get their cut, the veterans will get their Bonus, and FDR and you will get the credit."

General Butler pondered her comment. "You might have a point, Emma. You're a pretty smart young lady." He smiled. "Pretty smart."

-Chapter XV-

Meeting MacGuire

About a week and a half later, Emma received a call from her contact at the *Washington Daily News*. She was to call 'Mr. Gimlet' as soon as possible. Butler's efforts to maintain some level of anonymity amused Emma. She contacted him. He informed her that Gerald MacGuire had called and requested an urgent meeting at the Bellevue-Stratford Hotel in downtown Philadelphia. Late afternoon, Emma met Butler at City Hall and then walked south along Broad Street toward the hotel a few blocks distant. Soon the towering stone structure came into view.

"Pretty impressive," said Emma.

"Top of the line," said the General. "I hope we don't run into anyone I know. They'll be wondering why I'm there with a beautiful young woman." He laughed. They stood across the street from the hotel. "Before we go in, let's have an operational plan. Remember, you keep a low profile. I'll do the talking. You'll be my daughter, Ethel. You and I had an appointment for dinner, which I wouldn't cancel. So, you're tagging along. Got it?"

Emma smiled. "Seems simple enough. You think he'll clam up because of me?"

"Not a chance. We've had other conversations where my wife was in the room. This guy, MacGuire, is a strange bird. His conversation is all over the place. I assume it's because he got a head wound in the war. He won't pay any attention to you. His total focus will be on me. You'll see."

"Did he tell you what this is all about?"

"A matter of utmost importance." The General nodded. "Utmost importance."

"Great. I think we're about to hook the fish."

He smiled. "I'm ready to reel him in."

They crossed the street, climbed a set of stairs, and entered the massive and magnificent lobby. After checking in with the desk clerk, they were directed to a small conference room. When they entered, Gerald MacGuire popped out of his chair and greeted them with a smile. Butler introduced Emma to 'his daughter,' and they sat at a small conference table. MacGuire closed the door to the room and sat across from them. He was just as Jack had described him. His face looked like a sculptured sausage. Tiny droplets of perspiration clung to his forehead like translucent pimples. To Emma, he looked hot, pale, and unhealthy. She had detected a musty odor in the room, which she assumed he had produced. MacGuire made a pretense of acknowledging Emma at the table. Still, as Butler had predicted, he appeared to have little concern about her and quickly opened the conversation with the General.

"Well, I've been a busy man since we last talked, General."

"I got your postcards. You did some traveling," said Butler.

"That I did. But it was all business. I wanted to see how other countries treated their veterans. We know how they're treated in America, but you would be surprised. In Italy and Germany, the veterans are supported by the government...financially and otherwise. They find many ways to keep them busy and pay them for their services. It seemed clear to me that their former soldiers were always on call. Available whenever Mussolini or Hitler needed them. That's OK for them, but our boys over here wouldn't stand for it. Our guys are too independent. It's a different setup there."

"I would hope so. We're not a dictatorship," said Butler.

MacGuire nodded. "Right. Right you are, General. That's why I studied the situation in France. They're not a dictatorship either. But their veterans are very organized. They've got something called the *Croix de Feu*. It's run by this fellow, Lieutenant Colonel La Rocque.

Some kind of guy. Your kind of soldier. He fought in Africa until he was seriously wounded. They returned him to France. After he got back on his feet, he fought in the trenches. Now he heads up an organization of four or five hundred thousand Frenchmen. Veterans. These guys are dedicated to him and his cause. And they say he controls ten votes for every man in the organization."

"What do they stand for? Are they just trouble-makers?" asked Butler.

MacGuire lifted his hands from the tabletop to expose the palms of both hands, and then he shrugged his shoulders. "You know the French. They're all over the place politically." He chuckled. "But these ex-soldiers are patriotic. They're totally against the Commies. On that score, they're as American as any of us." He looked at Emma for confirmation.

She nodded gently with a hint of a smile.

He went on to talk about the political power of the *Croix de Feu* organization. He mentioned that they were part of the protesters in Paris who toppled the left-wing coalition. He explained that they were paramilitary and nationalist, but most importantly, they were an influential political action group respected by the politicians. He capped that discussion by saying, "This is the kind of veterans group that could be effective here...with your help."

"What's the bottom line?" asked Butler.

"We can use this kind of organization to support President Roosevelt."

Butler scratched the back of his head. "I didn't think that was on your agenda. Does he need that kind of support?"

"Sure." He nodded. "Sure. He needs all the support he can get. I think he'll go along with us now. He needs us. He's running out of money for his 'New Deal.' Our people are in control of the money. If he stumbles just a bit, the people will turn on him. Things could get out of control. We can help him keep order with our forces.

"Or maybe you just want to frighten FDR?"

"No. We want to sustain Roosevelt when others assault

him. The President is weak. He will come right along with us because he was born and raised in this class. And when he comes back, we've got the perfect solution. The man is disabled and overworked. He needs an assistant to take over the many heavy duties of his office. We'd set up a new position. Maybe something like a 'Secretary of General Affairs'". MacGuire smiled. "What do you think? Could you get your boys behind something like this?"

"I support democracy. I'm sure my 'boys,' as you call them, do also."

"That's the point, General. Everyone wants to support our democracy. But our country is in peril at this moment. The President's health is failing. Everyone can tell that just by looking at him. They would understand completely the need to support him. You'd be on the side of the angels. The five hundred thousand men you could represent would be on the same side."

"What about the veterans? And their bonuses? asked Butler.

"We figure ten dollars a month for the privates and maybe thirty-five a month for the captains just to be at the ready."

"That's a lot of money...."

Gerald MacGuire smiled and leaned back in his chair. "You've already met some of that money. Robert Clark has thirty million. I know he would spend half of that to ensure our country's protection. He's not the only one too. It's an unstoppable movement. General. Unstoppable."

Emma looked at General Butler. He appeared to be thinking it over carefully. Then he responded.

"Let's say I'm interested. But...I don't want to lead this organization."

MacGuire cocked his head and looked up. Then he returned his gaze to Butler. "When I was in Paris, my headquarters were Morgan & Hodges. We had a meeting over there. I might as well tell you that our group is for you to be the head of this organization. But the bankers are against you. The Morgan interests say that you can't be trusted, that you will be too radical, and so forth, that you are too much on the side of the little fellow. They do not want you. They say you'll get them together and then take them in the wrong direction. But our group tells them that you are the only fellow in America who can get the soldiers together."

General Butler just smiled before responding. "That's the story of my life, Gerry. I've gotten in a lot of trouble because I'm my own man".

MacGuire chuckled. "I get that. But those veterans would follow you anywhere. I told those people in Paris. You were the man." Then he went in the other direction and stared into the distance. "Maybe MacArthur. Some say FDR won't rehire him as Chief of Staff when his term is up.

Butler just scoffed and reminded him that MacArthur had attacked the Bonus Marchers in Anacostia. The veterans would never follow him.

"Well, then, we could get Hanford MacNider. The Morgan people want either MacArthur or MacNider."

"MacNider won't do either. He will not get the soldiers to follow him. He opposes the Bonus." Butler edged about in his chair as if he might get up. He checked his watch and looked at Emma. "Is there anything stirring about this project yet?" he asked.

"Yes. You watch; in two or three weeks, you will see it come out in the paper. There will be big fellows in it. This is to be the background of it. These are to be the villagers in the opera. The papers will come out with it."

"I don't follow. How is it going to happen?"

MacGuire answered. "We might have an Assistant President, somebody to take the blame, and if things do not work out, he can drop him. That is what we were building up Hugh Johnson for. But Hugh Johnson talked too damn much, and it got him into a hole. And FDR is going to fire him in the next three or four weeks."

"How do you know all this?"

"Oh," he said, "we are in with him all the time. We know what's going to happen."

The discussion ended when MacGuire said he would

soon be going to the American Legion convention in Miami to organize. He asked Butler to think long and hard about the position; he reiterated that he thought the General was the right man to lead the veterans. General Butler ended the meeting, excusing himself and 'Ethel", as he called her, saying that she had been very patient and they were overdue for dinner. They got up and left the man at the table. MacGuire tossed out a confident smile but then seemed to stare vacantly as they departed.

Once outside, they walked along the street, absorbing the fresh air and the sunshine. Emma proclaimed, "I am glad to be out of there, General. That man gives me the creeps."

Butler chuckled. "You see what I have been dealing with, Emma. At least he stumbled into the clear today. I am certain now that you are correct. They're planning a *coup*. We may have to drop a bomb on these people."

About two weeks later, Emma and the General spoke again on the phone. She had called him after reading a newspaper announcement about the new organization. It would be called the American Liberty League. Its primary purpose was to defend the Constitution, protect property rights and maintain traditional American values. The organization's founders included many political archenemies of Franklin Roosevelt: the du Pont brothers, John J. Raskob, the former head of the Democratic Party, and Al Smith, the former Governor of New York and a presidential candidate in 1928. Gerry MacGuire told the truth. A large and influential group had formed, possibly to remove or hinder FDR. MacGuire may also have foretold the impending political *coup*. Butler thanked Emma and told her that he would take it from here. He was going to enlist the help of some of his newspaper friends. Possibly they could corroborate the treasonous behavior and expose it to the public. Emma was satisfied that she had done all she could to stop it.

Finally, in November, a reporter named Paul French broke a story in the *Philadelphia Record* newspaper under

the headline "*$3,000,000 Bid for Fascist Army Bared.*"
Then on November 20, 1934, another newspaper article
declared that the House Committee on Un-American
Activities was investigating General Butler's allegations.
That night Emma and Jack celebrated their success with
an evening out at a cute, little D.C. café. With a fine bottle
of Bordeaux, they toasted to the truth. Finally, the news
had broken.

-Chapter XVI-

The Congressional Hearing

In mid-February 1935, Emma received a package sent by General Butler. She sat at the desk in the window bay of their apartment and used a letter opener to slice open the top of the plain brown envelope. The sun filled the room with light, and the radio played an Ozzie Nelson tune. She held a typewritten carbon paper copy of a document, maybe sixty pages long, bound with a clip. A handwritten note was attached.

"Emma,

Attached is an annotated copy of the House Committee on Un-American Activities report. This is a full report of the testimony that was taken by the committee. You will note the red-lined deleted words from the final report issued to Congress this month. I wanted you to see the entire testimony so that you can understand the plot's extent.

You won't find any mention of you in the document, which I'm sure will please you. I think the boys in Congress did a good job. Even though they left out some important names, the plotters have been publicly exposed and hopefully shamed into inaction. You know I brought in my old reporter friend, Paul Comly French. He went to New York and interviewed Mr. MacGuire in the Grayson offices. Our friend Gerry promptly spilled the beans and shot himself in the foot. Paul's testimony before the committee sealed the deal.

I think the rats have scurried back into their holes. I believe it is done. Thanks for your advice and encouragement. You are an exceptional person.

Your friend,

Smedley D. Butler, Major General USMC, Ret.

P.S. I read your article on the Bonus Marchers, which appeared in the Washington Daily News. Very good. Let's see if FDR gets my boys the bonuses they deserve."

Excitedly, Emma began to read the HCUA report, which was labeled as a preliminary public statement of findings and entitled "Investigation of Nazi Propaganda Activities and Investigation of Certain Other Propaganda Activities." It was dated November 24, 1934, and released by the two Congressmen who ran the committee, John W. McCormack and Samuel Dickstein. One of the first paragraphs was an eye-opener:

"This committee has had no evidence before it that would in the slightest degree warrant calling before it such men as John W. Davis, Gen. Hugh Johnson, General Harbord, Thomas W. Lamont, Admiral Sims, or Hanford MacNider.

The committee will not take cognizance of names brought into the testimony which constitutes mere hearsay.

This committee is not concerned with premature newspaper accounts, especially when given and published prior to the taking of the testimony."

Emma almost laughed to herself. It was as if the committee gave a warning that said, "Don't read this. You might get the idea that they were all in on the *coup* attempt."

The report then summarized the testimony of General Butler, Paul French, and Gerald MacGuire, and provided other documentation. The committee had wanted to get the testimony of the millionaire Robert Clark who had spoken with Butler about financing the *coup*. But Clark fled the country. The General's story was chronicled from when he was first visited by MacGuire and Doyle to later meetings where MacGuire had shown Butler $18,000 in thousand-dollar bills apparently to impress the General, and then to his most recent meeting at the Bellevue-Stratford Hotel. The details of this last meeting were accurately explained, and Emma was relieved to see there was no mention of the General's daughter or her. She continued to leaf through the document. The testimony of the reporter Paul French followed the General's testimony.

"French testified that he came to New York, September 13, 1934, and went to the offices of Grayson M-P Murphy & Co. on the twelfth floor of 52 Broadway and that MacGuire received him shortly after 1 o'clock in the afternoon and that they conducted their entire conversation in a small private office.

French testified under oath that as soon as he left MacGuire's office, he made a careful memorandum of everything that MacGuire had told him.

French testified that MacGuire stated, "We need a fascist government in this country to save the Nation from the communists who want to tear it down and wreck all that we have built in America. The only men who have patriotism to do it are the soldiers, and Smedley Butler is the ideal leader. He could organize one million men overnight."

Continuing, French stated that during the conversation, MacGuire told him about his trip to Europe and of the studies that he had made of the fascist, Nazi, and French movements and the parts that the veterans had played in them.

French further testified that MacGuire considered the movement entirely and tremendously patriotic and that any number of people with big names would be willing to help finance it. French stated that during the course of the conversation, MacGuire continually discussed "the need of a man on a white horse" and quoted MacGuire as having said, "We might go along with Roosevelt and then do with him 'what Mussolini did with the King of Italy.'"

Paul French's testimony was damning.

"He (MacGuire) emphasized throughout his conversation with me that the whole thing was tremendously patriotic, that it was saving the Nation from

communists, and that the men they deal with have that crackbrained idea that the communists are going to take it apart. He said the only safeguard would be the soldiers. At first, he suggested that the General organize this outfit himself and ask a dollar a year dues from everybody. We discussed that, and then he came around to the point of getting outside financial funds, and he said that it would not be any trouble to raise a million dollars. He said he could go to John W. Davis [attorney for J.P. Morgan & Co.] or Perkins of the National City Bank and any number of persons to get it. Of course, that may or may not mean anything. That is his reference to John W. Davis and Perkins of the National City Bank. During my conversation with him, I did not, of course, commit the General to anything. I was just feeling him along. Later, we discussed the question of arms and equipment, and he suggested that they could be obtained from the Remington Arms Co. on credit through the Du Ponts.

I do not think at that time he mentioned the connections of Du Pont with the American Liberty League, but he skirted all around it. That is, I do not think he mentioned the Liberty League, but he skirted all around the idea that that was the back door; one of the Du Ponts is on the board of directors of the American Liberty League, and they own a controlling interest in the Remington Arms Co. He said the General would not have any trouble enlisting 500,000 men."

MacGuire, according to French, expressed the belief that half of the American Legion and the Veterans of Foreign Wars would follow General Butler if he would announce the plan that MacGuire had in mind."

Next, Gerald MacGuire was put on the stand. There was considerable questioning by the congressmen regarding the financial details of the Committee for a Sound Dollar and Sound Currency. The investigators believed the organization was just a money-gathering front for the *coup* attempt. Ever the movie buff, Emma reflected on the coincidence of the 1990s Tom Cruise movie *Jerry Maguire* where Cruise, as Maguire, often used the expression "show me the money." And she thought about the 1970s movie, *All the President's Men*, a tale of the Nixon Watergate hearings, where the mantra was "follow the money." History repeats, she thought as she read MacGuire's testimony. The bond salesman weaved and bobbed his way through the grilling. A mental picture of the little fat man's balding head glistening in sweat popped into her head. But, with some conviction, he stuck to his story that he was only interested in getting Butler to serve as a proponent of a strong gold-backed dollar. And sometimes, in his testimony, he just seemed to lie outright. Emma knew because she had been a silent witness to his deeds.

"The Chairman. In August 1934, did you call General Butler on the phone and ask him if he could meet you in Philadelphia that afternoon? Did you, sometime in August, call him when you were in Philadelphia and ask him if he could meet you, and did you meet him at the Bellevue?

Mr. MacGuire. I think in August, I was going down on business to Philadelphia, and I called him and said I would be there and asked him if he was available and if he could meet me.

The Chairman. Did he meet you at the Bellevue?

Mr. MacGuire. Yes. He met me around 5 o'clock at the Bellevue-Stratford. I was there with him for about 20 minutes.

The Chairman. Did you talk to him about your trip to Europe?

Mr. MacGuire. Yes, sir.

The Chairman. And at that time, I think you were going down to your convention in Miami?

Mr. MacGuire. Yes, sir.

The Chairman. Did you tell him now was the time to get the soldiers together?

Mr. MacGuire. No, sir.

The Chairman. Did you tell him at that time that you went abroad to study the part that the veterans played abroad in the set-up of the governments of the countries abroad?

Mr. MacGuire. No, sir.

The Chairman. *Did you tell him that you went abroad and looked into the set-ups of the governments there and the part that the veterans played in Italy?*

Mr. MacGuire. No, sir.

The Chairman. *Under the fascist Government?*

Mr. MacGuire. No, sir.

The Chairman. *Did you say that they were the real backbone or background of Mussolini but that that system would not apply in America?*

Mr. MacGuire. *No, sir. The veterans were never mentioned when I met General Butler.*

The Chairman. *Did you tell him about going to Germany?*

Mr. MacGuire. Yes, sir.

The Chairman. *And that Hitler's strength in his organization was the veterans, but that that set-up would not go well in the United States?*

Mr. MacGuire. *I would like to tell you what I did tell him about Germany.*

The Chairman. *Please tell us.*

Mr. MacGuire. *I told him that, in my opinion, Hitler would not last another year in Germany, that he was already on the skids, and that from observations that I made over there, a number of organizations were against him, and to my way of thinking he would not last any longer than any other dictator would last. I did mention the fact also that I thought Mussolini was on the skids.*

The Chairman. *Did you at any time tell him about the set-up of the Hitler government and the part that the veterans played in that set-up?*

Mr. MacGuire. *No, sir. The veterans were not mentioned.*

The Chairman. *Did you tell him that you went to France and there you found the organization that "we were looking for "?*

Mr. MacGuire. No, sir.

The Chairman. *A super organization of all the veterans'*

organizations, of men who were noncommissioned officers and officers?

Mr. MacGuire. I will tell you how that might have come up. He asked me, "What did you find in France?" and I said, "Well, France is having a lot of trouble. They are trying hard to stay on the gold standard, and I think they will succeed." I said that I had had several talks with different people over there and had been very much interested in the economic picture of France and that different organizations and businesses were very hard hit because of the fact that they were staying on the gold standard. I told him that there had been an organization formed over there, an organization of veterans, men who were in the front-line trenches under fire, and I said that they are a very fine group, that they are with the Government and the people over there, and as far as I could see I thought France was all right. It was mainly economic my talk.

The Chairman. Did you talk with him about the forming of an organization of that kind here? Sir.

MacGuire. No, sir.

The later testimony of MacGuire related to his first meeting with General Butler brought a smile to Emma's face.

Question. Who rang the General to make an appointment and go over to his house, you or Doyle?

Answer. Well, I don't remember whether it was Doyle or myself.

Question. Was it the man by the name of Jack that rang and asked him for an appointment that you were two veterans and wanted to come over and talk to him?

Answer. Oh, yes; that refreshes my mind—I would like to get this on the record.

Question. Just answer that.

The Chairman. He says, "yes."

Question. Then, this Jack, what is his second name?

Answer. I don't remember his second name; he was

introduced to me in the Mayflower Hotel.

Question. That is Washington, and the call was from Washington?

Answer. Yes, I guess that is right."

Question. Don't you know who Jack was?

Answer. I don't know. Jack was introduced to me in a room in the Hotel Mayflower, and he was very much interested in forming a national veterans' organization and getting out a paper similar to the National Tribune; and he said he had been to see General Butler several times and he was a great friend of his, and I think either Doyle or myself said I would like to meet the General, and that is how the whole thing came up. This fellow said, "I will call him up and make an appointment." He said, "You are going back to New York, and you can stop there to see him." He called up from the Mayflower Hotel and made an appointment for us to see the General."

Emma laughed aloud at the audacity of her fiancé. Jack Travers' tiny butterfly wings gently massaged reality just enough to alter future events and change history, ending the *coup* attempt against President Franklin Roosevelt by some of the most powerful men in America. FDR had been saved.

-Chapter XVII-

Home Sweet Home

Together, Ethan, Zak, and Dr. A.C. Currant traveled ahead through time. No one could be sure whether it took an instant or a hundred years. Ethan's world was a swirl of activity, noise, and images as he experienced thousands of simultaneous hallucinations, all shattered into micro-snippets of time, too short and fast to comprehend. He couldn't understand the experience; he could only sense it. After previous travels, he and his fellow travelers had often talked about the transition period from one time to the next. There was no pattern to any of their memories, not even within the travel remembrances of an individual. Their explanations seemed only to be justifications for feelings of nothingness. It was as if their memories of time travel were a mysterious psychic soup, heavily seasoned with color, sound, and movement but leaving only a persistent and confusing aftertaste.

The three travelers had given themselves time to make the return train trip from Washington D.S. to Mystic Heights for their appointment with Currant's machine, the *TimeTravelle*. They were almost jubilant. They had foiled the attack on President Franklin Roosevelt. He would now be able to take his place in history. Ethan and Zak were sure the future would now be promising. Dr. Currant, ever the cynic, remained reserved. He had never believed in changing the past to fix the future. However, Ethan often reminded Currant that he had saved his brother's life as part of their time travel to 1963. Indeed this demonstrated the power of their actions. Currant would only say that this was a small and isolated example that happened to succeed in many ways. He still contended that their ability to successfully change the history of the world to achieve happiness for all was a potentially dangerous and untested theory. Ethan reaffirmed his belief that their return to the future would end this unresolved debate. Currant acknowledged that, but as he said, the future world might be so complicated that no one could know whether to call the time travelers' mission a success, a failure, or a non-event.

They had separated before their train arrived at the old train station in Mystic Heights, each getting off the train from different cars. Following their plan, each man took a different route to the top of the hill overlooking Smuggler's Cove. They paid close attention to make sure they were not followed. Their hike from the train station to the top of the cliff was arduous but uneventful. Their watches were synchronized. Ten minutes before "zero-hour," they popped out from their hiding places. Dr. Currant carefully surveyed the scene. The three time travelers stood atop the future home of Dr. Currant's concrete bunker. A stiff breeze blew in from the ocean. Pine needles and dust flared up as if anticipating the coming time travel turmoil. Currant first moved Zak into position. He adjusted Zak's feet until they were perfectly set. He did the same for Ethan. Then he moved into his spot. All was ready. He told them to stay motionless.

The second hand on Ethan's watch circled the dial as he took one more look at 1934. Randall Tower stood tall in the distance. The little town of Mystic Heights lay at the bottom of the hill, looking very cozy, a quintessential vision of a New England town. The people went about their business, driving their old automobiles and wearing their fedoras and flowered hats; they could only guess what the future would bring into their lives.

Ethan's last memory before leaving the year 1934 was the thought that his knowledge of the future was also uncertain. He knew he couldn't be sure of anything. Then the experience began. Suddenly, the machine grabbed him. He drifted from the past into the future like a corked bottle bearing a message of hope tossed into a raging sea. In no time, he washed up in the safe harbor of Currant's bunker.

The three men landed on the jump blocks. Ethan took a few seconds to shake off his flight's effects. He looked up. Zak was nodding at him. He was a pro now, thought Ethan, a veteran time traveler. Ethan returned the nod and checked out Dr. Currant. Maybe it was his age, but he was struggling with the experience. Even with all the modern preservation methods, Currant was still seventy-nine years old. Currant unraveled himself from the ball that his body had assumed on landing.

"You OK, Doctor?" asked Ethan.

Currant grumbled. "Hard on me. Give me a second. I'll be fine."

The three walked down the ramp into Currant's bunker. Ethan initially felt a sense of relief, but then he knew something was wrong. The mental cobwebs of time travel still clouded his thinking. He fought through the sensations and focused on his environment. He listened and looked carefully. "Something's different," he said quietly. "The lights are dimmer. I hear water dripping. Do you?"

Currant shook his head. "Can't hear much."

"You're right, Ethan," said Zak. "I hear it too."

They moved carefully through the room that housed the *TimeTravelle* and entered the lab. The lights popped on automatically, and Ethan's eyes adjusted quickly. He detected movement. Out of a niche in the wall, his father appeared. Jacques DuFour followed him into view. For a moment, no one spoke, then Ethan, his eyes wide with surprise, boomed out. "Dad. What the hell are you doing here?" His words reverberated off the concrete walls of the bunker.

His father rushed toward him, and he gave Ethan a firm hug. "I'm happy to see you." Then he pulled away and looked at Ethan as if he had never expected to see him again. "We have no idea what day this is. We heard the machine operating. We ran and hid. Thankfully, it was you. God, I can't believe you made it back." Warren Wright's eyes glistened with tears.

"Of course, we're back, Warren," said A.C. Currant. "I was in control this time. No screw-ups. No winter storms. No miscalculations. Just pinpoint accuracy." He laughed. "Dr. Currant, at your service."

"You misunderstand, Doctor," said DuFour. "We weren't sure if the machine would work."

Currant looked perplexed. "What?"

"What are you doing here? asked Ethan. "How did you even get in?"

"There is a hidden passage leading into the bunker. A.C. showed it to me years ago. He gave me the entry code." Warren Wright turned to face Dr. Currant. "Remember, A.C.?"

Currant's face had moved from a look of bewilderment to an expression of dismay. "Yes. I remember. But I also remember telling you that it was only to be used in an emergency."

Wright's face showed his emotion, and his voice was somber. "We've got an emergency, A.C., a bad one."

The three time travelers looked at each other.

"Let's sit," said DuFour. "You've come a long way. I'll make you some coffee."

"*Eso Que Ni Que*," exclaimed Zak.

Everyone except DuFour sat down at the conference table. DuFour provided drinks.

"Make mine a Johnnie Walker Black," said Currant. "You'll find it in the small cabinet."

Mr. Wright also skipped the coffee. DuFour poured, and he and Currant tapped glasses. "To the past..." said Wright as a toast, and they downed the whiskey.

For a few moments, they all relaxed until Ethan broke the silence. "Let's hear it. What's up?"

Warren Wright glanced at DuFour, then back to the three. He cleared his throat. "Something's happened. It happened not long after you left. Things changed. Neither DuFour nor I can make sense of it. We know you left, but we're not exactly clear about the why and what for." DuFour has some notes. "We've tried to put it all together. He thinks you left on a mission to change history. Maybe involving the second President Roosevelt." He paused. "That's a pretty good assumption. I would think."

"Are you kidding, Dad? You know we went back to save President Roosevelt. We left to make sure he stayed in office. And we succeeded."

DuFour set down his coffee mug and tapped his fingers on the table. "I'm sure it's all clear to you, but our view is a little foggier. I've checked into this as best as possible. There's not much to go on...."

"What do you mean? asked Zak. "Have you checked *The History*?"

"That's just it. Warren and I both have memories of such books. Government documents. But that's it. It's one of those things that you wonder if it ever really existed. We don't have it. I've looked around. I did find some history books I kept from years ago in the basement of my house."

"But, you teach history, Professor," said Ethan.

DuFour shrugged his shoulders. "I did. Years ago. But..."

"But what?" asked Zak.

"But, everything shut down. I've been retired for years." The Professor lowered his head.

"I hear you," said Currant as he looked at Zak and Ethan. "Well, fellows, this time we did it. We did change things. I can tell." He shook his head and turned back to DuFour and Wright. "And after listening to you, Jacques...maybe not for the better. You seem to me a little unsure of yourself. What about it, Professor? What's the state of the world? Things any better? History fixed? Or should we pack up and head back to the past?"

DuFour sipped a cup of coffee. "It's not that easy, A.C. I'll try to give you a quick rundown of the highlights."

"Fire away," said Currant.

"OK. I assume you're up to date on the facts before Franklin Roosevelt took office. Let's take it slowly. Alright?"

"We've got plenty of time," said Currant. "Walk us through it." He sipped his whiskey and smiled.

DuFour moved on. "Except for the period of World War I, America was an insular country. Focused on domestic issues. Willing to do business with other countries but unwilling to get involved with their intermural conflicts. We were a strong nation surrounded by peaceful neighbors and two great oceans. From the start, we claimed the land mass as ours. We believed in Manifest Destiny...from sea to shining sea. We pushed our borders to the max. Sometimes with brutality. Who can forget the Indian wars? But, most Americans remained more interested in protecting the homeland than acquiring and maintaining foreign colonies. We were isolationists. We had a distrust of big government and a belief in self-determination. America, the island fortress accountable only to itself. Maybe to a fault."

"That's what you taught us in history class," said Ethan. "But no matter, all that ultimately turned into MOM and her minions. Somewhere in time, that individualism got overwhelmed. The rules changed. You taught us that the presidential election of 2016 was the last one. President Swindell was assassinated. After that, the government created the ruling executive committee, and the country went over the edge. It never climbed back. The concept of MOM was created. Everyone was subject to electronic surveillance. Some cities turned into hellholes. Others like Mystic Heights seemed normal, but they were just brain farms. Training academies for the government service. Last year, we met a member of a resistance group. That guy, Vali, told us the population had been drastically and deliberately reduced. Nothing was like we thought. The world outside of Mystic Heights was a 'no man's land.' As a matter of fact, we left you with the pigeon that he gave us."

"I still have it," said DuFour. "I couldn't leave him behind. I've become quite attached. He's here."

"Well, that's something from the past...that remains," said Ethan. "Everything's confused now. Do you remember any of *The History* you taught us?"

"Cut us some slack, Ethan," said his father. "We have

never felt like this before. I'm not saying you caused it, but when you left, our lives changed."

DuFour shrugged his shoulders. "I suppose your memories reflect what I taught you. But our memories are weak. We can't build a coherent story about the past. I found some frightening student papers from years ago, written just before I was put out to pasture. They refer to false memories, the 'Mandela effect,' destructive memes, and fake news on the Internet. It's no wonder we're drawing mental blanks. The country was fractured in 2016. The music died, and so did *The History*."

"On the what?" asked Zak.

"The Internet. It's an electronic communications technology. As a matter of fact, eventually, it took over my job. Teaching at Cordwell and your old high school came to an end. Everything went 'online.' That's what they called the technology. That was years ago."

"What about the drones?"

"They're still here for sure. We saw a small one a few days ago on our way to the bunker. It didn't spot us. We made it in here. We were lucky."

"I can't believe changing one man in history can have such an effect," said Ethan. "It's crazy."

"History is a story, son," said Warren Wright. "It's a retelling of events. Events are interrelated. We know the authorities forbade time travel. It could be they were right."

"Jack said it was self-correcting," mumbled Zak. He seemed to be retreating into a shell.

"What?" asked Wright.

Zak stayed quiet, and Ethan answered for him. "I think he meant that no matter how events were altered, they would reassemble to maintain continuity and move toward an agreement. A consensus. An understanding of the past that everyone remembered and believed."

"Emma's Jack?" asked Wright.

"Yeah. That Jack," said Ethan. He cocked his head. "Ah. That's right. You don't know. Jack is a time-cop."

Currant rolled his eyes. "Emma saved that bit of news

until we arrived in 1934. You two weren't the only people dealing with change."

"How did you get away? Is Emma safe?" Warren Wright appeared to be on the edge of breaking.

"Don't worry, Dad. She's safe. Jack's an OK guy. He helped us. The two of them are living a good life in the old days. When we left, they had one more problem to solve."

"What's that?"

"There was talk of a *coup* to remove FDR from office. They had a plan to stop it."

"Well," said DuFour, "it must have worked. I read nothing of that. There is no way to know. But based on those old history books I found, it appears that after FDR had taken over, events changed significantly. I guess *The History,* if it existed, would be much different now. I am not sure if we had presidential elections after 2016 or if the country was then ruled by an executive committee. But in 2016, your man Swindell never showed up to be elected President. Donald Trump, an independent populist, won that election, creating great rancor. He ran as a Republican, but he was never truly accepted by those in power. Not even the congressmen and senators from his own party. His presence was terribly disruptive to the established two-party election system and the ongoing war economy. Then the entire economy collapsed. It was like a second Great Depression. President Trump didn't cause the collapse, but apparently, he was blamed by the news media and other politicians."

"How long did this fellow Trump serve as President? asked Ethan.

"He was assassinated on election night. Killed before he had a chance to celebrate his win. He was the last president. The country floundered. Almost another world war. The judicial system struggled to make sense of everything. Then the United States of America just disintegrated. The country broke apart. Texas, Florida, California, and New York seceded. The other states congealed into regional boundaries. I think Russia forcibly reclaimed Alaska. It was a mess."

"What about FDR?"

DuFour continued. "When FDR first took office, the people believed in him. He was a virtual dictator. Then over the years, he tried every trick in the book to pull the country out of the Great Depression. He expanded the government considerably. But the economic problems didn't end. They continued until the war ended. He served four terms. Well almost. He died while in office during his last term in the middle of World War II."

Zak appeared confused. Ethan could tell he was having a tough time dealing with the revelations. Zak interrupted. "Four terms. That would put him in office through 1948."

"He died in '44," said DuFour.

"OK, but you had said World War II was still going. I remember that an armistice was signed in 1941," countered Zak.

"If that was ever a fact, it is not anymore," said DuFour. "The war ended in 1945. Unconditional surrender. It was a brutal war. Eighty million people, maybe more, died. This time the whole world was in on it. We got attacked by Japan and...."

Ethan rubbed his chin. "Zak's right. You taught us. The war ended in 1941. The Germans occupied France. England and Germany signed a peace treaty. I think the Germans pulled out of France in 1942. We never entered the war. Things settled down." He shook his head. "I don't remember Japan at all."

"Actions have consequences, guys. Eighty million dead. Damn..." mumbled Currant. He poured another drink for himself and Warren Wright. "I think we need another. This is not going well."

"Things are very different now, Ethan," said DuFour. "I'm sure your memories are correct, but events must have changed with FDR in office,"

"They say he changed the face of government," said Wright. "The 'most influential President of the Twentieth century...right, Jacques?"

"Apparently, he did. He introduced America to some

new concepts. 'Big government' was one of them. He also increased the power of the Executive branch. In doing so, he changed the checks and balances of the system. In time, over the next decades, Congress evolved into a corrupt, political eunuch. The Judicial branch ignored the massive power the Executive had created. The Executive branch got stronger and stronger. Presidents were declaring states of 'emergency' at will. For the last thirty-three years...ever since 911...the country has been in a 'state of emergency.'"

"911?" asked Ethan.

"A serious terrorist attack," said DuFour. "That set the tone for the next three decades. Presidents issued Executive Orders which overrode the entire constitutional process. Some of my student's work claimed they even created an Executive Order forbidding the President and Congress from reading any other Executive Orders. They created another government within the government. One operated completely in the dark, controlling its military forces, influencing governments worldwide and the U.S., and operating under an unknown budget. The money to support this 'deep state' as some called it, was stolen from other programs or rubber-stamped by Congress in ignorance of the amounts or purpose. Or maybe created by dirty side-businesses like drug-running and human trafficking. And the 'on-book' economy was based almost exclusively on war and killing. The American people, the corporations, and the politicians all ran on war."

"It looks to me that after we had won World War II, we entered into what was called a 'special relationship' with England. Both countries wanted to control the world. The Brits needed our muscle, and we needed their skills. Combining the 'deep state' and the need to keep the wars going for our economic survival became a permanent condition. After World War II, America was almost continuously at war. Korea, Vietnam, Iraq, Kuwait, Libya, Syria, Iran, Egypt, and Ukraine. I can't remember them all. But after the economy died in 2018, the country went to the dogs. The war came home. People split up. Took sides. Two opposite political factions attacked the government and each other both politically and with guerilla warfare."

"This is all because of FDR?" asked Ethan.

"It appears to have started with him," said DuFour. "Fact is, I'm guessing on much of this. But it's the best I can do. You can judge for yourselves. Things just began to move in another direction after FDR took office."

"This is not good," said Ethan. He looked at his father. "I'm tired. Let's go home, Dad. I'll bring you up to date on Emma. Maybe this will all make more sense in the clear light of morning."

Warren Wright gave his son a sympathetic look. "Can't happen, Ethan."

"What?"

"That world is gone. I'm sorry to tell you. It's all gone out there. Our homes. Our friends. It's a total madhouse. We were lucky to find our way into the bunker. At least we can survive in here."

Currant stood. "That's it. That's the cork in the bottle. I told you we shouldn't have been fooling around with history. You guys and Emma have screwed things for everyone." After this pronouncement, he paced the room, mumbling to himself. The others at the table sat mute.

-Chapter XVIII-

Erasing the Future

The time travelers realized they were drained. Their energy had been sucked out by the excitement of the last few days and the process of time traveling. Ethan, Zak, and Currant were too exhausted to continue their circular discussions about the causation of historical events and the world's fate. Warren Wright and Jacques DuFour were sympathetic and suggested they get some sleep. Currant's lab had a sleeping room that looked like a submarine's bunk area. Currant and Ethan took the lower berths. Zak grudgingly agreed to the top bunk. They all fell into deep and restorative sleep in a few minutes.

Ethan awoke to the smell and sounds of bacon and eggs frying. He arose and stumbled half-asleep into the kitchen area.

DuFour, who had a reputation as a food buff, was working the stove. He smiled at Ethan. He stroked his goatee. "Quite a nap. It's been almost ten hours," he said. "Sit, *mes amis*. I've made a four-cheese omelet for you with some bacon on the side."

Ethan, still groggy from the long sleep, nodded without speaking. He sat on a stool and carefully sipped from a cup of coffee. Slowly, he shook out the cobwebs in his mind and returned to the land of consciousness. "Wow, I must have been tired."

"You had quite a shock. In addition to the rigors of time travel, you've had to deal with an epic paradigm shift. Warren and I have had some time to digest it, but you, my friends, have been slapped in the face with reality." He poured Ethan a glass of orange juice.

"Thanks, Jacques," said Ethan, who was well into his meal.

Warren Wright walked into the kitchen wearing a big

smile. "Hey, sleepyhead. You're looking fit. The 'zees' did the trick, eh?"

Ethan sucked up a half-glass of the juice before replying. "They did, Dad. I think I'm coming to grips with our situation now. It's a bitch, isn't it?"

"That it is. But I remember what we used to say when I was in the Bureau. "Everyone has problems.""

Ethan rolled his eyes. "Seems rather harsh."

"Maybe," said Wright, "but when you're a cop, you realize that the world...any world...is not perfect. There are always problems, and there are always solutions. Our job now is to make some decisions and move on. The world as we knew it is gone. It's not coming back."

Ethan dropped his head. "Seems like we screwed up big-time."

"Maybe. Maybe not. I'm not certain we ever knew what was going on. That was the problem. We just guessed based on *The History* as presented and propagandized by the powers that be. Or should I say 'the powers that were.' We played the game with the cards we were dealt. But it was a crooked game."

"*Mon Dieu*, it was just a story," said DuFour. "We know that. It was a story designed to control the masses."

"In school, we enjoyed your telling the story, Professor. You made history live vividly in our innocent minds."

"Thanks, Ethan. Wherever we are at this moment, it is my doing. Not yours. I was the one who encouraged you to attempt to resurrect John Kennedy. And then Franklin Roosevelt. I should have known better. Changing one man in history, no matter how great the man, will not alter the course of the historical river. What will be...will be."

"Maybe it's just a game," said Ethan.

"What do you mean?" asked DuFour.

"I mean, what if all of this. All of us. It could be just one big supercomputer simulation. Someplace, someone wrote a program that created our world, including every one of us. Didn't you ever sense that everything fits together a little too neatly? That the delicate balance of forces is dictated by game parameters built into the system. History always seems to self-correct consistently even though humans supposedly have free will. Our time travel attempts to change future events never worked as we wanted them to. Maybe they're programmed to fail. Maybe free will is just an illusion."

Ethan's father sat down on the stool across from Ethan. "It may be that we have free will. But my experience in law enforcement taught me that people are very predictable. When push comes to shove, they usually rely on their reptilian brain. Flight or fight. I think there are special people. People with the vision to change the course of the river of history. But the mass of people from all stations in life, unfortunately, revert to the mean. That's just the way it is."

"So what? JFK wasn't willing to fall in line. Therefore, he was taken out. And what about FDR? He didn't seem to fit either. His ideas were very radical. But he was successful. He did change history."

Wright smiled. "You time travelers gave him a chance. You gave him several. But, I have a feeling. Even though he was a strong man. And an exceptional politician. In time, the system and the flow of history probably chipped away at him. The world above this bunker might be the failed result of his good intentions and honest effort. We'll never know."

Ethan downed the last bite of this omelet and took another sip of coffee. Then he looked across the table, first at his father, then at DuFour. "However you look at it. It is just a big game. Computer simulation. Divine construction. Or just a lucky roll of the genetic dice of creation. It's a game. It's life. Life to be lived."

"Could be, Ethan. Could be. I doubt we'll ever figure that out," said his father. "We gave it our best shot. Now we have to move on."

They heard rumblings from the sleeping room, and Zak and Dr. Currant appeared. "What's this about moving on? asked Currant.

"I was just saying. We have to make some decisions," said Wright. "Sit down. Have some breakfast, and let's get going. The world above is nuts. Fortunately, at least we have this quiet place to decide our futures."

"Amen," said Zak.

They chatted at the table for the next fifteen minutes and finished their breakfast. Ethan was the first to attack the problem. "OK, what are we going to do? Options?"

Currant answered. "Options.... short term we can stay here. I think it's still safe from prying eyes. But while we have plenty of well water, we'll run out of food in a couple of weeks. Realistic options? One, we locate the resistance movement and join forces with them."

"You mean our old friend Vali?" asked Zak.

"There's probably an array of resistance groups, but he's part of one. And he knows you two."

"The second option?" asked Warren Wright.

Currant smiled. "Personally, I prefer this one. But I don't want to influence anyone. For me, I would return to the year 1934 and live out the rest of my life in the past. We still have the *TimeTravelle*. We could be back there tomorrow. You and Ethan would be reunited with Emma. Zak, you would just have to make sure to keep your *Voicenator* in a safe place. And Professor, I'm sure if I can survive the trip, you can. You'd be living in history. What better place for a history professor? I rest my case."

No one spoke. Warren Wright nodded. "I'm with you, A.C. We have nothing to gain by staying in this world. It seems to be going down the tubes. I haven't experienced the 1930s, but if nothing else, they'll provide a taste of personal freedom. I'd welcome the opportunity. And I wouldn't mind watching my grandkids grow up."

"Do you know something that I don't, Dad?" asked Ethan with a smile.

"I know human nature, son."

"What about you, Professor?" asked Dr. Currant.

"I have nothing or no one to keep me here. I'll do it."

"Zak?"

He looked at Currant. "You still have those old 1960s *Wall Street Journals*?"

Currant nodded.

"Well, then we won't starve," said Zak. "But I'm getting some terrible vibes from the world above. It's time to go." He scratched the top of his head. "It's our only real option. *Eso Que Ni Que!*"

They all looked at Ethan. "I'm in. But one thing. I think we should invite our friend Vali. He saved our lives. He deserves to join us."

Currant rubbed his chin. "That would make six of us. The machine has only four positions."

"Would it work?" asked Wright.

"We'll do it in two trips. But how do we contact Vali?"

"That's easy," said DuFour. "We still have Marconi."

"Who?"

"The pigeon that Vali gave us. Through all the violence and terror, I managed to keep him safe. His home is here. We can send Mr. Vali an invitation on the wings of our good friend Marconi."

"Then it's settled," said Currant. "We're off to 1934. And we will never return."

Over the next few days, they planned their trip. DuFour was in charge of devising long-term money-making schemes. Currant had important digital files he had saved in preparation for his many trips. DuFour worked through those files and interviewed Currant, Zak, and Ethan. In this way, he compiled a list of investment positions to guarantee income for the group. In addition to the horse race and stock results for the next thirty years, Currant still had a significant amount of gold, currency, and synthetic diamonds in his vault to act as seed money.

Warren Wright took on the task of creating credentials for himself and DuFour.

Ethan had released Marconi, the homing pigeon, with a message inserted into a tubular metal container attached to the bird's leg. They didn't expect the bird to return, but the instructions explained their plan and required Vali to meet them at the top of the hill at Smuggler's Cove in four days. They knew the bird would return to its roost and would be found by Vali if he was still alive.

Currant's plan was simple. The travelers would be transported by the *TimeTravelle* in two trips. Before the final trip back to the past. Currant would arm the demolition charges he had strategically placed around the underground bunker. Not long after that, the time travelers would land in the world of 1934. The top of the hill and Currant's lab and time machine would be blown to bits leaving only speculation as to the cause of the blast.

"One more thing," said Currant on the first day of preparation. "I will need DNA samples from each of you."

"What for?" asked Ethan.

Currant laughed. "Proof of death. We're going to disappear. I want the authorities to find enough DNA material after the explosion to enable them to identify us. Or at least to be certain that somebody died in the explosion." He retrieved four plastic sample tubes from his lab coat and directed everyone to fill them with spit. He marked each to identify Wright, DuFour, Zak, and Ethan. "Warren, you and the Professor can continue your work. I'm going to show these two how to make an organ. "Come with me, fellows. I'll show you my cloning lab."

Ethan and Zak followed Currant down a long hall where they entered a special lab devoted to replication. It was a gloomy place filled with giant machines and equipment. Ethan sat at a table that held several large vats filled with fluid and interconnected with tubing and wires. Backed up to a wall, several electronic devices were stacked. Zak peered into the vats. One held a rack submerged in clear bubbling fluid. A familiar human nose and two ears rested on the stand.

"Those are done. Mine. They're just seasoning at this time. See the resemblance?" He held his finger to the tip of his nose and leaned back to capture the light.

"That's your schnozzola, Doctor. I'd know it anywhere."

"Come here, Zak. Stand behind Ethan. You'll be like the Tin Man. I'll make you a heart."

Zak took his position while Currant worked his magic, inputting Zak's DNA sample into the replicator machine. "This won't take long."

They watched the large tank on the table in front of them. Currant carefully filled it with three different liquid chemicals, then capped the top and activated the electrodes. Ethan nervously watched as Currant created a new heart for Zak. He was a bit squeamish about the process. Over the next fifteen minutes, a heart organ grew like a ripening tomato. It might not have been a perfect likeness to Zak's heart, but its DNA would match. If any searchers found a tiny bit of this cloned organ, they would, upon scientific analysis, be satisfied that Zak Newman, 23 years old, a resident of Mystic Heights, had died in a massive explosion.

"You're the Wizard of Odds and Ends, Doctor," said Zak. "Thanks for the new heart. I'll give it to my next girlfriend."

"Sorry, Zak. You'll be dead. Or at least your heart will."

On the fourth day of preparation, they were ready to go. Dr. Currant released a surveillance drone. Together they watched the monitor as the small drone and camera flew over the hill and made successive passes along the cliff overlooking the bay. Vali had saved Ethan and Zak's lives a year earlier and had shown them a secret passage from his underground tunnel system. This passage opened onto the bay and could be accessed only at low tide. They searched the base of the cliff wall, around the hill, and at the designated meeting place on the hilltop. But there was no sign of the man.

"He's not there. And he's nowhere in the area. I'm afraid your friend Vali is not coming. I'm going to send the drone to the outer perimeter. I just want to check." Currant flew the drone skillfully. As it passed over Mystic Heights, the time travelers hardly recognized their hometown. Burned-out drone cars were scattered in the middle of streets and up on sidewalks and lawns. Garbage and debris were strewn everywhere, and houses burned, leaving charred gaping holes in their roofs. And no people appeared.

"What happened?" asked Ethan. "It looks like a bomb hit the town."

Warren Wright commented quietly. "It's been raped, guys. More than one mob worked its way across town looting, burning, and killing."

"What about our house?" asked Ethan.

"You don't want to see it, son."

"I'm going to cruise around." Currant directed the drone to fly over the edges of town and brought it back. "Look!" The screen showed a line of government vehicles approaching via the truck bypass route. They're heading this way! We have to go. It's time," said Currant.

"Can't we wait a little longer?" asked Ethan.

"No, I've already set the charges. We're packed and ready to go. And we've got company coming. Let's do it!"

They all wore suitable 1930s clothes that they had selected from Currant's closet of wardrobe props. Warren Wright, Jacques DuFour, and Zak donned their yellow safety goggles. Handshakes and well-wishes followed. The three took their places at quadrants on the platform. In the center of the circle, they stashed several bags that contained equipment, money, and information.

Currant and Ethan hid behind a protective screen. The machine began humming at the pre-set time. Very quickly, the sound increased to ear-splitting levels. Ethan had never witnessed the action of the *TimeTravelle* from the sidelines. He was excited as he looked into his father's face, then DuFour's. Terror was overtaking them. But Zak, the veteran, was smiling at them, maybe to comfort them, or maybe as bravado. "*Hijole!*" shouted Zak. And then, they were not. The machine's noise died down, and the underground space was a tomb.

"We're next. We go in two minutes. I told them to clear the area immediately on landing. Let's go," directed Currant. The drone was still in the air. The aerial images showed the white U.N. vehicles were about a half-mile from the entrance to the road leading up the hill to their bunker. "No time to lose. They're closing in on us," said Currant. He pushed the call-back button on the drone. The drone turned, and they were surprised to see a bird ahead in the camera's view. It appeared to be a pigeon.

"Is that Marconi?" asked Ethan.

"That would explain the invasion force heading our way. They're tracking the bird." Currant tapped a switch, and the screen went dark. "Get onto the machine, Ethan. There's no time to lose!"

A.C. Currant and Ethan gathered their bags and walked up the ramp of the *TimeTravelle*. After tossing the bags in the center circle, they took opposite sides, leaning into the cold steel slabs. Ethan listened to Currant as he bid goodbye to his machine. He put his fingers to his lips and then transferred a kiss to the steel plate behind him. They waited in silence. Ethan knew that the entire lab and the top of the hill would be obliterated five minutes after their departure. If anything went wrong, there was a kill-switch nearby that either of them could push. But that wouldn't be necessary. The machine hummed quietly at first, then louder and louder. Ethan had made the trip many times before, but the excitement never ceased. He looked at Currant, his eyes were concealed by the safety goggles, but Ethan saw tears. This was the last trip for both of them.

They stood perfectly still. In the seconds before departure, Ethan was relaxed and confident. He knew they had made the correct decision. He, Emma, and everyone else would live peacefully in a new time and place. They would start new lives. They would live in a world of reality far removed from the mind-numbing, privacy-depriving, inhuman future technology. The time machine screamed. Ethan took a deep breath. He felt a slight vibration in the metal plate behind him. Then he was gone. At that moment, he no longer existed.

-Chapter XIX-

The Beginning

*"Get a drone up there, and put a net on that bird. I want it in one piece. Over." The lieutenant clipped his walkie-talkie to his belt and strolled to the cliff edge. A salty light rain peppered his face. The ocean, lost in a mass of low gray clouds, could only be heard. Directly below, the waves broke and receded relentlessly against the rock face. The repetitive sound of their crash and return was almost hypnotizing. It was a moment for him to reflect. He guessed this area at the top of the hill overlooking Smuggler's Cove had been some kind of park or monument. Pieces of stone, which had obviously been worked, dotted the destruction. They looked like parts of stone columns. He felt like an archeologist examining an ancient civilization's ruins. It was his civilization, but he knew very little about it.

He looked back at the robocops sifting through the rubble and wondered how different he was from these mindless hunks of metal and plastic? At least he had a position. He was a ranking soldier in the United Nations forces. He had to consider himself lucky. His parents abandoned him soon after his birth in the early years of the twenty-first century. His survival, his entire existence, had hinged on a random event. An old woman vagrant had heard the baby version of him crying. She had been scrounging through a dumpster behind a private dining club, and his muffled cries reached her ears. The sound must have triggered something in her. Somehow this woman had retained her sense of humanity. Carefully, she dug deeper into the decaying remains of uneaten food and restaurant garbage and found the source of the audible pain. She pulled him out of his smelly crypt, placed him into the bottom of her shopping cart, and returned to the barrio.

He became her reason to live, struggle, and exist; the two barely survived. In time, the infant became a toddler, and the toddler became a young and valuable boy. Although the stakes were very low, amounting to her survival in a world that didn't care, her gamble had paid off. She lived, and he thrived. He was industrious, as only the young and desperate can be. He quickly became a cunning and dangerous street person.

Most importantly, he had good genes. By the time he was sixteen, he was six feet three inches tall and weighed over two hundred twenty pounds. About a year after his surrogate mother had died, he was picked up in the regular police round-up. They were looking for men to battle the resistance, and he was looking for a future. They turned him over to the UNKP, the United Nations Keepers of the Peace, and he was inducted. Rigorous training had turned him into one of them. They strengthened him with a program of diet, exercise, and chemical and biological enhancements, all the while hammering in psychological programming, along with weapons and tactics training. The UNKP was the ultimate governmental authority for all the territory, formerly the United States of America. The purpose of this organization was twofold: protect the elite, and extinguish all dissent. Two branches evolved with these two different assignments. The lieutenant was a member of the Cooperation and Redemption Corps, which maintained a continuous investigation process, entrapment, and elimination of all the guerrillas, dissenters, street criminals, public complainers, and useless people incapable of sustaining their lives. He had risen through the ranks and distinguished himself by uncovering a vast local network of tunnels operated by a ragtag rogue army. Now, he was an officer. He was one of them. But, a part of his mind remained his alone.

He still had his thoughts, although he kept them to himself. He wondered why he bothered to think about the future. What had happened to the world? Occasionally, he captured men and women who spouted out their crazed ideology. They found it necessary to give him their insight and reflections on the past he had never known. They rattled on about freedom, righteousness, justice, and the pursuit of happiness, confident that they could make a better life for everyone if someone would just listen to them. But that was not something he could do. All such people were immediately bound, gagged, and taken to the nearest Resolution Center. It was as if the ideas and dreams buried in these lost souls were the most dangerous aspects of their being.

But, in time, the lieutenant was able to piece it together. His bosses were right. The enemy was the people; they were all mentally defective, beyond repair or rehabilitation. They were too dangerous to keep alive, and thus, in the end, their existence had to be resolved permanently. But their numbers were dwindling. His job might be on the line. Then what? He knew the answer. The elite and entitled would be protected by the robocops. They would be fed, serviced, and provided for by other robots. The window was closing on ordinary humans such as him. But, if he was determined and lucky, possibly he could prove himself to be more valuable than the others soldiers and the robocops. He might be promoted to work in Intelligence. He might have a future. That was his goal and only hope.

"Lieutenant!" shouted someone behind him.

He slipped out of his reverie and turned to face the young soldier.

"We got the bird. This message was on this leg." The man handed him a small piece of paper.

He read the message: *"We're taking the last train out of Dodge. We have room for one more. Meet us at the top of the hill above the cave entrance at high noon six days before the next full moon—Your former frozen friends, ever thankful. E & Z"*.

He reread it several times and then smiled. It was important. It gave him hope for the future. Carefully, he placed the message in his wallet.

"Is the bird still alive?"

"Yes, sir."

"Good. Put it in a cage and bring it back to me. And don't mention a word of this to anyone. Got it?"

"Yes, sir."

-Chapter XX-

What's Past is Prologue

A small white clapboard church, its ambitious copper-clad spire piercing the bright blue sky, stood proudly atop the grassy hill overlooking the city of Washington D.C. Today, the church's emotional heartbeat countered the agonizing, threatening rumble of the Great Depression. Joyously, amidst the early morning sun, the bells rang loudly. Their cry was intended to chase away evil spirits and promote the wishes of all true believers in the magical powers of the marriage ceremony. It was the ultimate special day for Emma Callan-Wright. Dressed as a princess and beaming excitedly, she held her father's arm as they slowly walked up the aisle. In 4/4 time, the organist played one of Emma's favorite songs, "As Time Goes By," as if it was the march of time.

Both sides of the aisle were lined with guests. Their presence surprised and pleased Emma as they came into view. She nodded regally to General Butler and his wife. He acknowledged her with a friendly military salute. She knew that his battle against the evil forces had ended in a tie, with FDR in office and the exposed plotters humbled but retaining their influence and power. The time travelers' efforts had saved Roosevelt's presidency. Emma was filled with pride knowing this great man, Smedley Butler, had chosen to join their wedding celebration.

In the next pew, she spotted John and Mary Sweeny. Their three children squirmed excitedly as the Princess Bride passed. Emma had not seen the Sweeny family since that fateful, fiery night on the Anacostia Flats in 1932. Little Michael had grown into a sturdy young man. His sister Brenda, dressed in her Sunday best, blushed when Emma smiled at her. Adjacent, filled with the wings and energy of youth, their sister Colleen stood on the pew, her tiny hands grasping its top rail as if in anticipation of an amusement park ride. Emma's brush with death two years ago during the destruction of the Bonus Marcher camp was long forgotten. But seeing little Colleen, Emma immediately recalled the bravery of an immigrant named Branko, who had saved many lives that night while losing his own. In retrospect, he had, with his actions, preserved freedom in America. In her heart, he was here today.

Ahead, Emma's soon-to-be husband, Jack Travers, waited. Tall and handsome, he looked like a movie idol. More so than anyone, he was taken by Emma's beauty and grace. She locked onto his eyes for a moment. They smiled. Then she glanced sideways at the others. Jack had invited several people that he knew from working with Mrs. Roosevelt. Of course, the President's wife could not attend. That would raise too many questions. But Franklin Roosevelt's loyal valet, Irvin McDuffie, and his wife formed the head of a row of people who worked directly or indirectly for the Roosevelts. Emma was honored to have them in attendance. In a pew close to the front, her comrade in arms, the quixotic A.C. Currant, stood proudly. Beside him was Margaret Dougherty, the woman he now described as the love of his life. She guessed soon they too would be husband and wife. Deep down, she knew that old A.C. was a hopeless romantic. Standing next to the couple, her loyal friend Zak looked at her and made a face, a strange signal of friendship, to which Emma responded with a brief scowl and followed with a quick, broad smile. A few more measured steps brought her into the arena of love. She separated from her father, Warren Wright, and left him with a kiss.

She took her place beside Jack. Her maid of honor, Dorothea Lange, was a professional photographer whose work was recognized by Eleanor Roosevelt. The combination of Lange's powerful black and white images and Emma's poignant prose had given Mrs. Roosevelt, a woman of the American aristocracy, great insight into the plight of the ordinary people. Of course, Ethan, the best man, stood tall, defending the right side of the altar. To Emma, he was as solid as a giant oak tree. With one quick glance, she bonded again with her twin. His eyes seemed to say, "let's get this over, Sis." She knew he never was a big fan of pomp and circumstance, but this was her big day, not his. And she was enjoying every moment.

The preacher called the assembly to order. In a simple ceremony, the eternal words were spoken by Emma and Jack—two people from another time and place. These two renegades from the future now danced on the stage of current reality. They were elated, not only because they would be together forever but also because they knew that everyone had made the correct decision. They would experience life in a time and a place that offered the most humanity, possibility, and freedom ever experienced by anyone in history. The joy of this understanding was electrifyingly expressed in the embrace and kiss that followed the preacher's announcement to the world that she and Jack were now man and wife. And the people rejoiced and celebrated this new beginning.

—THE END—

TIME TRAVEL TWINS
W. Green

SAVING JFK
Volume 1
The Twins attempt to stop the Chicago
assassination of JFK in November 1963, and create
a better future for their world of 2028.

X-OOMING FDR
Volumes 2, 3, 4
The Twins travel into danger and intrigue.
Determined to redesign history and the life of a
man who is only a footnote in the history books of
the 21st century,

SAVING TRUMP
Volume 5
The year is 2016, and the Twins and Zak team
up with their descendants, Samantha and Jason
Keene, during the presidential election. Donald
Trump is in...but does he continue?

BOOKS BY OTHERS RELATED TO THE EVENTS DESCRIBED IN X-ooming FDR

The Bonus Army: An American Epic by Paul Dickson and Thomas B. Allen. Published by Walker & Company, 2004.

War is a Racket by Major General Smedley Butler. Published by World Classics Books, 2010.

Since Yesterday: 1929-1939 by Frederick Lewis Allen. Published by Bantam Books, 1961.

B. E. F.: The Whole Story Of The Bonus Army by W.W. Waters and William C. White. Published by Cincinnatus Press, 2007.

The Last of the Doughboys: The Forgotten Generation and Their Forgotten World War by Richard Rubin. Published by Houghton Mifflin Harcourt, 2013.

The Five Weeks of Giuseppe Zangara: The Man Who Would Assassinate FDR by Blaise Picchi. Published by Academy Chicago Publishers, 1998.

The Outfit: The Role of Chicago's Underworld in the Shaping of Modern America by Gus Russo. Published by Bloomsbury, 2001.

Since Yesterday: 1929-1939 by Frederick Lewis Allen. Published by Bantam Books, 1965.

The Plots Against the President by Sally Denton. Published by Bloomsbury Press, 2012.

<u>The Chicago Outfit</u> by John J. Binder. Published by Arcadia Publishing, 2003.

<u>When Capone's Mob Murdered Roger Touhy</u> by John W. Tuohy. Published by Barricade Books Inc., 2001.

<u>Florida in the Great Depression</u> by Nick Wynne & Joseph Knetsch. Published by The History Press, 2012,

<u>The Plot to Seize the White House</u> by Jules Archer. Published by Skyhorse Publishing, 2007.

<u>It Can't Happen Here</u> by Sinclair Lewis. Published by New America Library, 2005.

<u>FDR's Deadly Secret</u> by Steven Lomazow, M.D. and Eric Fettmann, Public Affairs, 2009.

<u>Devil Dog: The Amazing True Story of the Man Who Saved America</u> by David Talbot with Illustrations by Spain Rodriguez. Published by Simon & Schuster, 2010.

Thanks for Reading
X-ooming FDR 1934
Did you like the book? Your on-line book review
will really help the author get the word out.